Deserts of the Dragons

Dragon Shifter Romance

Mac Flynn

All names, places, and events depicted in this book are fictional and products of the author's imagination.

No part of this publication may be reproduced, stored in a retrieval system, converted to another format, or transmitted in any form without explicit, written permission from the publisher of this work. For information regarding redistribution or to contact the author, write to the publisher at the following address.

Crescent Moon Studios, Inc.
P.O. Box 117
Riverside, WA 98849

Website: www.macflynn.com
Email: mac@macflynn.com

ISBN / EAN-13: 978-1975952426

Copyright © 2017 by Mac Flynn

First Edition

CONTENTS

Chapter 1..1
Chapter 2..8
Chapter 3..15
Chapter 4..23
Chapter 5..30
Chapter 6..36
Chapter 7..41
Chapter 8..48
Chapter 9..55
Chapter 10..67
Chapter 11..75
Chapter 12..81
Chapter 13..89
Chapter 14..95
Chapter 15..100
Chapter 16..108
Chapter 17..117
Chapter 18..124
Chapter 19..132
Chapter 20..139
Chapter 21..146
Chapter 22..152
Chapter 23..160
Chapter 24..165
Chapter 25..174

Chapter 26	179
Chapter 27	188
Chapter 28	193
Chapter 29	198
Chapter 30	207
Chapter 31	214
Chapter 32	224
Chapter 33	229
Continue the adventure	237
Other series by Mac Flynn	242

DESERTS OF THE DRAGONS

CHAPTER 1

The beautiful sky above me. The green forest and fields below me. A handsome dragon lord behind me. Everything was perfect.

Well, almost perfect.

"Do we have to fly all the way to the desert!" I yelped.

Xander winced. My arms were wrapped tightly around his neck and my body was pressed close against his chest. "You did not wish to ride," he reminded me.

I glared at him. "I have a tender bottom, okay? It wouldn't have taken a two-week trip. Besides-" I leaned back and admired his chest, "-not all the view is a terrifying death."

Xander smiled. "I am glad I could be of service."

I caught a peek over my shoulder at the woods far below us. They were the outlying forest of Thorontur, King of the Arbor Fae. There was also a little bit of green plains that represented Xander's dragon territory.

I cringed and looked back up into Xander's face. "You know, have you ever thought about bringing over a plane or car from my old world?"

Xander shook his head. "It is forbidden to bring any mechanical devices through the Portal."

My eyes narrowed at him. "What about that truck that drove me over?"

"That is an exception."

"Uh-huh. How about we make another teensy-weensy exception and I get a private jet?"

He blinked at me. "A 'jet?'"

I rolled my eyes and settled into his arms with my own crossed over my chest. "Never mind. So where are we going again?"

"To the outpost city of Almukhafar where we will travel by land over the desert to the city of Hadia wherein lies the Temple of the Priests of the Portal."

I arched an eyebrow. "Why don't we just fly across the desert?"

"You just expressed dissatisfaction in flying."

I shrugged. "Yeah, but I hate sand in my shoes more than I hate heights."

Xander looked ahead and pursed his lips. "The wings of dragons are incapable of withstanding the heat of Rimal Almawt al'Abyad. From Almukhafar we must travel by beast of burden to the Temple. Fortunately, it is only a journey of two days."

I cringed and rubbed my posterior. "Goodbye, soft butt cheeks."

He slyly grinned at me. "I might offer to massage them for you."

I snorted. "And I might take you up on that offer."

Spiros flew up beside us. His eyes twinkled with mischief. "I will gladly do my part to bring you comfort, My Lady, and offer to massage one of your cheeks."

"Captain Spiros!" Darda scolded him as she flew up behind we three.

"I will be the comfort for my Maiden," Xander assured him.

I raised an eyebrow at my dragon lord. "Don't I get a say in this?"

"No."

My eyes narrowed. "Listen, *partner*, on the rest of this steerage-class trip I will be the only one to massage my derriere."

Xander lifted his head and looked out over the horizon. A small smile crept onto his lips. "There is no need for that."

"Why?"

"Because we have arrived."

I whipped my head around to face forward. The green horizon abruptly stopped, and beyond the straight line was an endless stretch of white. The midday day sun illuminated the white sands and created a near-blinding display of light.

I blinked hard against the brilliance. "Please tell me you guys have invented sun glasses."

Xander chuckled. "You will grow accustomed to the sun's bright light, but let us continue."

We flew the few short miles to the vast expanse of sand and touched down on the edge of a small city. The small metropolis was laid out in a grid pattern with narrow dirt streets between large blocks of buildings. Most of the city lay in the green grass of the straggling plains, but a few blocks stretched into the desert. The structures closest to us were built from the trees of Thorontur and rose two stories over the grassy plains. The houses in the desert were simple single-story buildings made of mud bricks.

People crowded the streets. Their skin was the color of soft brown maple leaves in the fall, and their attire was light and airy to handle the hot winds that blew off the desert. Many wore broad-brimmed hats of dried grass and carried fans of wood to cool themselves.

Many peddlers pushed narrow carts through the streets and shouted their wares to passers by.

"Fish! Get your fish! Caught in Alexandria only five days ago!"

"Pots! Pans! All that you could ever desire!"

"I have here the finest merchandise this side of the Potami. On sale today! Do not miss what I have to offer!"

Xander grasped my hand and smiled down at me. "Shall we?"

I grinned. "Let's do this."

We joined the throngs of people in the streets with Darda and Spiros at our backs. I was hit by a variety of pleasant smells that bespoke spicy food and roasted meat. Other smells weren't pleasant, and I found out what those were when someone leaned out an open second-floor window. They placed a pot on the sill and tipped it. The contents of a day's worth of waste dropped splattered onto the streets.

I cringed and pressed closer to Xander. "Lovely place. Remind me to book a vacation house sometime."

DESERTS OF THE DRAGONS

Xander swept his eyes over the area. "Do not think the less of the city. The outpost of Almukhafar is a very ancient city that has found it difficult to change some of its ways."

"Anything else I should be worried about?" I wondered.

He pursed his lips. "One cannot be too careful in such a place. There are many foreign travelers, and a simple matter of murder could be overlooked."

I felt the color drain from my face. "M-murder?"

Xander smiled down at me. "Do you believe I or any of us would allow such a fate to befall you?"

Spiros glanced to our right. The ground floor of some of the buildings opened into shops and taverns. Some unscrupulous characters leered at me. The captain laid his hand on the hilt of his sword and the men looked away.

I frowned at Xander. "I can protect myself, too. You're not the only dragon I've got, remember?"

"Your water abilities are limited here," he pointed out.

I looked around. There wasn't a drop of liquid. My shoulders fell. "What I wouldn't do for a fire hydrant. . ."

Darda set a hand on my shoulder and smiled at me. "Let us pray to the gods you will not need our protection."

We reached a large square. Stalls were set up around the perimeter, and in the center was a large well. The vendors sold everything imaginable. Fruits, vegetables, animals of various sizes from mice to horses. Spices hung from long ropes, and tradesman advertised their clothing on thick pieces of wood.

The local women in their brightly-colored garb gathered around the well to exchange gossip. Men bartered and haggled at the stalls. Apprentices and shop boys scurried to and fro with delivery bundles under their arms.

"My Lord! Miriam!" The familiar voice came from the thick crowd of women gathered around the well, and soon a familiar sus emerged. It was Tillit. He strode over to us with his usual sly smile on his lips. Tillit took one of my hands in his and pecked a light kiss on the back of my hand before he raised his eyes to mine. "Might I saw you have grown lovelier than last I saw you, My Lady." Xander cleared his throat. Tillit released my hand and straightened. "Have you only just arrived?"

"We have, but we do not intend to stay long," Xander told him.

The sus looked from me to Xander and back. "Looks like I caught you just in time. You're headed for the Temple, right?"

Xander nodded. "We are, but what brings you to the Temple? I was not aware you traded in pilgrimage goods."

Tillit snorted and waved a hand at Xander. "I've never touched the stuff, especially around that place. You can never tell when a dissatisfied customer would come back asking for a-" he paused and shuddered, "-refund."

"What are pilgrimage goods?" I spoke up.

The sus jerked his head over his shoulder at a line of six stalls. They all sold small figurines of naked women in dervish-style poses or seated like a Buddha. The women wore wreaths of grass around their heads and their expressions were friendly.

"Those are statues of the Alumu Aleazima, or Great Mother for those who don't speak Altinin," he told me. "She's the protector of merchants and desert wanderers, so you can see why she's so popular around here."

I swept my eyes over the busy trading area. "Why are there so many merchants this close to the desert?"

DESERTS OF THE DRAGONS

"Almukhafar is the last city before the desert, but beyond the sands in the southern part of the continent are many ports," Xander told me.

"And there's also the Temple," Tillit reminded him. "They run a pretty good business supplying the pilgrims who go there looking for blessings and to get a look at some of those books in that library the priests have." His eyes flickered to Xander. "But I'm sure you're not here to be bamboozled out of some of your gold, My Lord. Did something north of here get you down here?"

Xander arched an eyebrow. "You are referring to the incident at Bear Bay?"

I blinked at them. "Bear Bay?"

Tillit grinned. "Nothing gets past you, does it, My Lord? Anyway, you're right. I was there when it happened, and it's left me with a couple of questions I want answered."

"Such as?"

"What happened at Bear Bay?" I asked them.

The sus glanced around before he lowered his voice and leaned toward us. "Such as how a human was able to get into our world *without* using the Portal." Xander frowned. Tillit studied him. "You look like you've heard this before, but not from Bear Bay."

"What happened?" I spoke up.

"Tell us what you can," Xander ordered him.

Tillit grinned and jerked his head down a narrow alley. "If you'll just step into my shop I'll answer both your questions."

CHAPTER 2

Tillit led us into the narrow alley and out through the other side. We were on a smaller side street to the busy thoroughfare that led to the main square. Smaller, grimier shops without open fronts lined both sides of the streets. An occasional blacksmith shop with their dirty work bellowed on the street corners. The clientele of the street walked quickly and with their eyes ever one everyone else.

Tillit guided us to a small establishment that was two floors. The lower floor was a tavern without windows. Candles on the walls lit the few round tables in the place, but the corners were shrouded in darkness. A short bar ran the length of the back wall. The bartender didn't even look up from cleaning a glass when we entered. We plopped ourselves down at the table farthest from the door. The tavern was empty besides us and the unaware bartender.

DESERTS OF THE DRAGONS

Tillit set his arms on the table and leaned forward. His voice was low and his eyes flickered over all of our expectant faces. "Bear Bay lies in the far northeast of the continent. It's a nice trading city, but-" he wrapped his arms around himself and shuddered, "-they can keep that cold weather."

"What of the portal?" Xander insisted.

Tillit's face fell. "I didn't actually see it myself. A woman-" his eyes flickered to me, "-a human woman found it."

I raised an eyebrow. "A Maiden?"

Tillit shook his head. "Nope. She was just a normal human who stumbled into our world through a portal."

"Did she know how the portal came to be created?" Xander asked him.

He leaned back and clasped his hands together over his ample stomach. "Nope. All she knew was she was in the human world one moment and then ours the next. She told me where the portal dropped her into our world, but when I went looking for it I couldn't find a trace of it. It was like it was never there."

Xander pursed his lips. "Were any Bestia Draconis or portal priests spotted in the area?"

Tillit arched an eyebrow. "No, but you think there should've been, don't you?"

My dragon lord nodded. "Yes. Only a Bestia Draconis or a reckless priest would risk both our worlds to open a portal."

I frowned at him. "My dad-" Xander shot me a warning glare, but it was too late.

Both of Tillit's eyebrows raised as his eyes fell on me. "What's this about your dad?"

I shrank beneath Xander's hard glare. "Maybe. . ." I squeaked out.

Tillit leaned toward me and studied me with his sharp eyes. "How'd you happen to find out about your dad? I heard you were orphaned pretty young."

Darda leaned forward to block Tillit's view of me. She glared at the sus. "You pry too much into the affairs of others, young man."

Tillit grinned. "That's my job, ma'am, and I do it well."

The feet of Xander's chair clattered across the floor as he stood. "If that is all the information you can give us about the incident, we really must be going."

Tillit stood and smiled at Xander. "I'm in a bit of a hurry myself to get to the Temple, so how about I tag along with you, My Lord?"

Xander's narrowed eyes flickered to me and his tone was tense. "You may so long as you ask no questions."

The sus placed his hand over his heart. "I promise on the grave of Humble Hubert I will not ask any questions."

I frowned, but Xander nodded. "I will accept your promise. Now we should go."

Xander led the other two out of the tavern. I stayed behind with Tillit and glanced at him. A sly smile graced his lips. "Herbert really isn't dead, is she?"

He leaned toward me and lowered his voice to a whisper. "Let's just say that Herbert's decided to go on a long vacation away from the attention her name evokes."

I jerked my head at Xander's back. "Does he know that?"

Tillit straightened and shrugged. "I don't know, but he took it and I won't betray his trust. I'm honest, and honesty is Tillit."

DESERTS OF THE DRAGONS

I raised an eyebrow. "So you're not going to ask me any questions?"

He shook his head. "Nope. However-" his eyes flickered to me. He leaned in close and winked. "-that doesn't mean you can't tell old Tillit what you know."

"Tillit."

The color drained from Tillit's face. He straightened and cleared his throat as he looked ahead of us. Xander had stopped and stared at us over his shoulder. "Yes, My Lord?"

"I would appreciate if you didn't encourage my Maiden to betray herself to the authorities, should they overhear you," Xander told him.

Tillit bowed his head. "As you wish, My Lord."

Xander continued onward. I followed, but my curiosity was aroused. I glanced at Tillit. "What's he mean by that?"

The humor in Tillit's face had vanished. He pursed his lips and shook his head, though his eyes never wavered from the back of Xander's head. "I can only guess, My Lady, but when Tillit finds out you'll be the first to know."

I frowned, but didn't purse the matter further. That's because the houses thinned and the street opened. The shadows of the narrow roads vanished and were replaced by the scorching orange light of the sun. A pair of men leaned against the base of a cluster of tall palm trees, and behind them in the leafy shade were a half dozen large animals.

It was a cross between a camel and a jackal, a combination I never would have thought possible if I hadn't seen them with my own two eyes. The beasts were smaller than a camel but larger than a jackal. The creatures had the same tan and brown short fur of the jackal, but a single short hump rose from its body. A short, bushy tail whacked at the flies that agitated its rear. The long-snouted heads were attached via a long neck. One of the things yawned and I saw two rows of sharp teeth. They pulled at their ropes and dug into the sand with hard hoofs in the shape of paws.

Xander approached the men. They stood and bowed to him with wide smiles on their faces.

One of them stepped forward. "Good morning to you, Your Lordship. We hope your journey was well."

Xander nodded before he looked past him at the beasts. "Very well, thank you, my dear friends Tajir and Tabie." The men's smiles widened at the familiarity. "I assume you received my message?"

Tajir bobbed his head. "I did, Your Lordship. The animals have been packed as you requested." He stepped aside and gestured to four of the beasts. They had leather bags slung over their rears just behind the hump. Two skeins of water connected by rope hung around the animals' necks. "You shall not have any problems crossing the desert, but-" his eyes flickered to Xander and he held out his hand to the dragon lord, "-there is the matter of payment."

Xander drew out a small purse and plopped the bag into the man's palm. The bag jingled with the sound of many coins.

Tabie hurried over as his leader opened the purse. They were all smiles as they admired the payment. Tajir tucked the purse into his pocket and bowed. "It is always a pleasure doing business with you, Your Lordship."

"And with Tillit," Tillit spoke up. He wound through our group and bowed to the beast merchants. "I hope you haven't forgotten about my request."

The merchant gestured to a fifth animal. It, too, was outfitted for the long desert ride. "Your beast is ready as well. On payment, of course."

"Of course," Tillit agreed as he drew out a few coins and gave the man the money. The sus turned to us and smiled. "It seems we're destined to be together, my friends."

I looked back to the animals. "Together with what exactly?"

"They are alkalb muhadab, the beasts of the deserts," Tajir told me.

"And that means?" I wondered.

He smiled. "That is 'humped dog' in your tongue, My Lady, but you may call them hadab if that so pleases you."

Xander glanced around the area. Other than our group and the two traders, there was no one else around. "It appears there are fewer hadab merchants than I have seen in the past."

Tajir's smile wavered. A shadow crossed over his bow. "You are correct, Your Lordship. Many of the hadab have already been taken for the Jame, but many of my brothers will not sell our beasts to lone travelers who are unfamiliar to us because of the rumors."

Xander arched an eyebrow. "What rumors?"

The merchant pursed his lips. "There are rumors of raids upon the caravans where the bandits appear from beneath the sands. For that reason we will not trade our beasts to strangers for any amount of gold."

"Can no one describe what happened?" Xander asked them.

Tajir shook his head. "No, Your Lordship. There have been no survivors."

Tabie leaned toward his comrade and whispered into his ear. "The lights."

Tajir glared at him. "Do not be so foolish as to believe those stories, Tabie."

"What lights?" Xander wondered.

Tajir sighed and shook his head. "My companion has heard stories of small suns that roam the high mountain of Hadia after dark. For that reason, many in the city will not go up there after the sun has set."

Xander bowed his head. "I see. Thank you for the information." He turned to me. "Are you prepared?"

I glanced at the creatures. They moved with the grace of an arthritic calf. I winced and rubbed my derriere as I looked to Xander. "So more riding?"

He nodded. "More riding."

My shoulders slumped and my face fell. "Oh goody. . ."

CHAPTER 3

"Ow. Ow. Ow."

My assessment of the hadab's movements wasn't far off. The beast I rode rocked me in four different directions, and sometimes all at the same time. My posterior was sore from the hard saddle, and the hump at my back was as comfortable as a bag of bricks.

My mantra made my dragon lord smile. "I still offer you my lap if you wish for greater comfort."

I glared at him and tightened my grip on the reins. "I said I was going to ride one of these things on my own, and I mean it."

The said creature added its comment with a heavy spit as it rocked back and forth in its quick trot. I glared down at the strange beast that I burdened. It leisurely looked ahead of us with its sharp canine eyes.

Spiros laughed. "It is said the hadab keeps its friends and remembers its enemies. Perhaps it considers you an enemy."

I looked ahead and raised my chin in the air. "Maybe the spitting means the opposite." The animal snorted. The party laughed. I shrank down in my saddle and glared at the beast. "Thanks a bunch. . ."

Tillit followed behind our group. He leaned forward in his saddle and raised his jolly voice. "So, My Lord, you know what brings me to the Temple, but what of you and your merry band?"

Xander didn't look around when he replied. "Miriam must see the world."

The sus snorted. "You're more secretive than usual, My Lord." His eyes flickered to Spiros. "What say you, captain? Do you need to see the world, too?"

Spiros smiled and shook his head. "No, Master Merchant, the world needs to see me. I cannot hide this wonderful face from the world forever." Darda and I rolled our eyes.

Tillit laughed and slapped the horn of his saddle. "I applaud you, captain. That's at least a better lie than the one your lord gave me."

"What I said was not a lie," Xander insisted.

Tillit wagged his finger at Xander. "Then you should know better than to tell half a truth, My Lord. What will your Maiden think?"

I frowned at Xander. "I think he needs to tell his Maiden why she can't talk about certain things."

The sus leaned to one side to catch Xander's gaze. "We are out in the desert. No one can hear you but us and the desert scorpions."

DESERTS OF THE DRAGONS

I glanced down at the sand. A breeze swept over the small grains and shifted them. "And maybe the thieves. . ." I murmured.

Xander pursed his lips and I noticed his hands clenched his reins until the knuckles were white. Finally he sighed. "Very well, since we are alone."

Tillit grinned. "That's the lord I know! Know what have you got for Tillit?"

Xander stopped his hadab and half-turned so he could look Tillit in the eyes. "Miriam visited Valtameri in his ocean domain and he allowed her to glimpse her earliest memories."

Tillit grinned and winked at me. "Good for you!"

"One of them was of her father creating a portal."

Tillit's eyes widened and his face drooped. He whipped his head back to Xander. "You're pulling my tail!"

Xander closed his eyes and shook his head. "If only that were true, but you see why this must be kept a secret."

Tillit whistled and nodded. "Yeah. If that got out she'd be in big trouble."

I whipped my head from one to the other. "Why would I be in big trouble?"

Xander turned his attention to me and pursed his lips. "If what you glimpsed was true then your father committed the gravest of sins of our world. The justice demanded of such an act would invariably be demanded from his daughter."

I frowned. "But I didn't do anything! I couldn't even talk to tell him not to do it!"

"That's the rub with the portal," Tillit spoke up. His face was tense as he looked at me. "The priests get to be the ones to investigate, and they don't like having competition."

"Or anyone ending the world," Darda spoke up.

Tillit's eyes flickered to her. "If that's what you think would happen, you go on believing that. I'm a pessimist by nature, but that huge portal the lords have used-pardon me for saying, My Lord-it hasn't done a dang thing to destroy our world, and that thing's been around a long time."

Darda glared at him. "The Portal is well-maintained under the watchful eye of the priests. If anything was to go wrong they would have the ability to close the Portal."

He jerked his head at me. "I'm not saying I don't trust Apuleius with Miriam, but because she's Xander's Maiden he wouldn't get a say in all this. The same might be said of Cayden's guy, so would you trust her to the rest of the big priests and their underlings? Especially the Inquisitors?" Darda pursed her lips, but said nothing. Tillit leaned back and furrowed his brow. "That's my sentiments exactly, so I'm not going to be arguing with My Lord's request to keep my mouth shut about it."

I turned to Xander. "What exactly would they do to me if they found out?"

Xander sighed. "They would investigate the matter, and during the investigation they would capture and use your memories as evidence."

I started back. "They would what?"

Tillit leaned on his saddle horn to be closer to me. "The priests have a nasty habit of using their magic to delve into peoples' minds for information."

"Without their permission?" I guessed.

He nodded. "Yep, and whatever you felt with Valtameri browsing through you, you wouldn't like it if someone started rummaging around in there-" he nodded at my head, "-without your permission."

"I will not allow such an assault," Darda spoke up. She straightened in her saddle and glowered at Tillit. "They shall not touch My Lady."

He held up his hands and smiled at her. "And I agree with you there. I'm just telling Miriam what they'd do to her if they found out."

Xander lifted his reins as he looked over our small group. "I do not believe the danger would come from anyone here, but we must all be vigilant. The Bestia Draconis have followed ahead of us through a number of our adventures, and we must assumed that they have already arrived at the Temple."

He turned his hadab forward and we continued onward. The mood was soured by our dour conversation. I would have brooded if it was in my nature, but there was no sense letting possibilities get me down.

I pulled up beside Xander and looked up into his tense face. "So back there with those two guys, one of them said something about a 'jam' thing that was going on right now at the Temple. What's that about?"

"Jame is the pilgrimage of the faithful to the Temple," Xander told me.

I wrinkled my nose. "Then they're what? Worshiping the portal priests or something?"

Xander smiled and shook his head. "No. They worship a goddess who predates the portal priests."

Tillit lifted one of his water skeins and raised it in a toast to the desert. "Good ol' Alihat Dhahabia. She hasn't failed me yet."

I blinked at him. "Who?"

He winked at me. "She's the big girl around here. Alumu Aleazima rules over the desert, but without Alihat

Dhahabia there wouldn't be anybody around here. Her names means the Gold Goddess, and she's the one in charge of water and life. The locals pray to her so their wells never to run dry and they get lots of kids." He drank a little water and poured a few drops out onto the desert floor. "As I always say, a little praying to the local god never hurt anyone."

I turned to Xander. "So is she a fae?"

Xander shook his head. "I cannot say. There are tales of the faithful meeting a radiant woman who blesses them with water, but no one I know has personally met her. If she is a fae than she is very ancient for her worship goes back into the times before dragons ruled this area. The humans were said to worship her, as well."

"And the dragons decided she wasn't so bad and adopted her as their own," Tillit chimed in as he trotted up to my side.

"So how did the priests get the Temple?" I asked them.

Tillit chuckled. "They didn't ask for it, that's for sure. Apuleius and the rest of 'em are nice guys, but some of their predecessors weren't so polite."

Both of my eyebrows shot up and I whipped my head to Xander. "They stole it?"

The dragon lord pursed his lips as he stared ahead of us. "It is a blemish on our history, but yes, the priests with the aid of their dragon lords took the Temple and

"But they didn't get their library," Tillit reminded him.

"Was it that great?" I wondered.

He nodded. "Some of the legends say it was almost as good as the Mallus Library."

I furrowed my brow. "That sounds familiar."

"That is the same library you found in the castle," Darda reminded me.

DESERTS OF THE DRAGONS

I looked over my shoulder and grinned at her. "The one you led me to, right?"

She smiled in return. "The very same."

"Can I finish my story?" Tillit spoke up.

"Continue on with your story of woe, Storyteller," Spiros teased him.

Tillit sat straight and cleared his throat. "As I was saying, the dragon lords besieged the Temple. Since neither side could fly it was a war of archers and hadab cavalry. Those in the Temple dug themselves in for a long fight and lasted for a month before their supplies began to run low. They feared the lords would find their water source and thirst them out, so one of them came up with a brilliant plan. They would lose their Temple, but in revenge the priests would never have the books."

I cringed. "Fire?"

Tillit grinned and shook his head. "No, something far more cunning. One of the men, a former sailor in his early youth, devised a-" Xander made a sudden stop. Our party stopped with him.

We stood at the top of a small sand hill. Below us stretched an endless floor of glistening yellow desert. To the far right and many miles away was a long row of orange cliffs. To our right and in front of us was nothing.

I looked at Xander. "What's wrong?"

He nodded at the distance. I leaned forward and squinted into the distance. Tall shadows skidded across the length of the bowl. I pointed at them. "What's that?"

Xander looked past me and at Tillit. There was a devilish grin on the dragon's lips. "The end to Tillit's story." The sus's shoulders drooped and he frowned. Xander returned his attention to me. "Would you like to see?"

"Does it mean I can get off these things when we get there?"

"Yes."

A grin slid onto my lips as I leaned forward over the animal's neck. "Then let's hurry up."

CHAPTER 4

I kicked my heels into the animal's sides and was nearly dismounted. The awkward trot of the camel transformed into the smooth sprint of the jackal. I fell forward and wrapped my arms around the smooth neck of the creature as we careened down the hill. The reins fell from my hands and hung loose in front of the hadab's chest. My hair blew behind me and strands whipped at my face.

"Stop! Stop, you stupid animal!" I yelled.

Xander came up on my side. He sported a wide, devilish smile on his lips. "Would you like some assistance?"

I glared at him. "I'd like to get off this thing!"

He leaned down between us and grabbed my reins. A quick pull back and my beast slowed to its rough trot. I pushed myself into a seated position and wiped away the strands of hair.

"Why didn't anybody warn me that that button does that?" I growled.

The rest of our group caught up with us. Spiros had the same teasing smile as Xander. "My Lady, I have never seen a riding style such as yours. Do you have a name for it?"

Darda frowned at him. "That is quite enough from you, captain. Do you not know she could have been maimed or killed?"

Spiros chuckled. "Our Lady would not allow such a beast to do her in." His hadab threw its head back and snorted. Our group broke into laughter. Even I cracked a smile. Spiros patted the side of the beast's neck. "I meant no offense, my friend."

Xander trotted a few steps ahead of us and nodded at the dark shapes on the horizon. "Shall we continue?"

We continued our journey across the sand dunes toward the mystery. As we grew closer I could make out that there were a half dozen large shapes some twenty to thirty feet high. They looked like narrow rafts that curved down on either side and were attached to large water skis. Each had a single mast in the center with a large sail attached to it. The flapping cloth seemed to mimic the winding heat waves that arose from the desert floor. A mess of ropes led from the sail to a single upright post in the back. I didn't see a rudder.

A couple dozen men moved around the rafts. Some tightened the ropes, others lashed the posts tighter together with ropes. One of them looked up and turned in our direction. He pointed at us and shouted something unintelligible. The others leapt to their feet and swung around to face us with their hammers and long, curved short swords.

DESERTS OF THE DRAGONS

Xander stopped us ten yards from the group and held up his hands. "Tahiati, friends."

One of the men stepped forward. He looked to be about eighteen with sandy black hair and piercing brown eyes. His skin was darkened and leathered by the rough environment, but he stood tall and wore a chain of gold tightly wrapped around his neck.

He raised a hand. "Tahiati, friend. What brings you to us?"

Xander smiled and nodded at the strange boats. "We merely wish to look at your wonderful miraj. They are very well made."

The young man bowed his head. "I and my men thank you for the-"

"You should really drop the elegant talk. It doesn't suit you," Tillit spoke up. All eyes turned to the sus who leaned over the horn of his saddle and grinned at the leader. "How have you been, Sinbad?"

The young man grinned at the sus. "I was better until I saw you were in their company, Lord Sus. I thought I could trust these newcomers-" he swept his arm over us, "-but I see that with you among them they cannot be counted on to hold a pebble."

Tillit chuckled. "Oh, you can trust them, but I don't know if they can trust you." He nodded at the weapon-bearing men behind Sinbad. "I don't think you've ever given some visitors such a warm welcome."

Sinbad looked over his shoulder at his men. "There is no need to worry. You may resume your work." The others lowered their weapons and turned back to the sailing vessels. He returned his attention to us and bowed. "My apologies if I startled you. I meant no disrespect."

"Sure you did," Tillit teased as he slid off his hadab. He led the animal over to Sinbad and looked over the rafts. The sus rubbed his chin and nodded. "Not a bad group of miraj. You might place this year. That is-" he glanced at Sinbad with his eyes twinkling, "-you don't crash again."

Sinbad stretched himself to his full height which was nearly a head taller than the sus. "I will not crash. I have sworn to Alihat Dhahabia and Alumu Aleazima that I will place the leaf upon their alters of my home and bring glory again to our village."

Xander slid off his hadab and looked the young man over. "You are Sinbad of the oasis of Rimal Talamue, are you not?"

Sinbad turned to Xander and nodded. "I am, but I do not know your name, friend."

Xander bowed his head. "I am Xander of Alexandria, and these are my traveling companions."

The young man's eyes widened. His imposing manner shrank a little before the shadow of my dragon lord. "Xander, Lord of Alexandria?"

Xander smiled. "I hope my being a lord does not change our new friendship."

Sinbad gathered himself and shook his head. "No, but you must know that being a dragon lord brings you no great perks here. The desert and its sands rule over this region."

Tillit laughed and patted Sinbad on the shoulder. "You forget how much older My Lord is than you, young dragon. He was skiffing across the sands side-by-side with your father."

The young man arched an eyebrow and took a step toward Xander. He tilted his head a little and his sharp eyes studied my dragon lord. "You knew my father?"

DESERTS OF THE DRAGONS

Xander nodded. "I did. He was a fine Alfurasan Alriyah. I hope to see that you have inherited his gifts."

Sinbad straightened and gave him a crooked grin. "I would very much like to test my skills against yours, Xander, Lord of-" Xander held up his hand.

"I am Xander to my friends, so I would like you to call me that," Xander requested.

The young man walked backwards and gestured with one hand to the boats behind him. "We shall see if we are still friends after a race, dragon lord." The challenge caught the attention of the men behind him and everyone stopped their work to listen. Sinbad jumped onto one of the vessels and grabbed hold of a rope that ran down from the top of the mast. He leaned forward and let the rope hold him in the air. "That is, if you accept my challenge."

Spiros glanced at Xander. "My Lord, I believe the whelp means to be thrashed."

Sinbad grinned. "There is no glory without danger, unless your lord here does not face danger."

Xander closed his eyes and chuckled. "I would rather not, but I accept your challenge and shall let my wings speak for me."

Xander removed his shirt and revealed his wings. Their long shadows stretched across the sands and engulfed our small group. The eyes of the men behind Sinbad widened and many whispered among themselves in their native tongue.

Sinbad smirked at Xander. "Your long wings will not assist you here, dragon lord, as you will soon find out." He stooped and pressed his palm against the ground. Everyone was quiet as they watched him. His smirk widened as he stood and swung around to face his men. "Prepare the two fastest miraj, and quickly! We race this day!"

A cheer went up from the men and they hurried to finish the final preparations on two of the rafts. They closed the sails and lashed the ropes tight to the rear poles.

Xander claimed one of the crafts for himself while Sinbad hopped aboard the other. The weathered lad removed his shirt and allowed his wings to push from his back. His leathery wings were half the length of Xander's, but the skin was twice as thick. He flexed them with an agility that made one think they were another pair of arms or legs. They curled up so they were nearly perpendicular with his body, or they tucked in so the bottom tips tickled his sides.

I looked to Darda. "Why are his wings so short?"

"The heat of the desert meant the dragons could never fly, so their wings are now short and useless," she explained.

Xander crouched down at the pole with its mess of ropes and folded his wings against his back. They looked so delicate compared to those of Sinbad. He grabbed the ropes in one hand and held onto the pole with the other.

Sinbad did the same and glanced at Xander. "Once around my ships and back here should be plenty of exercise for you, old dragon lord."

Xander smiled. "I will endeavor to keep up with your youth."

I turned to Spiros. "So what exactly is going on?"

"They mean to race across the sands in those two miraj," he told me.

"So how do they sail without water?" I asked him

He tilted his head back and nodded at the sky. "They sail on the winds and the narrow runs slide over the sands."

DESERTS OF THE DRAGONS

I looked from left to right. The desert was as calm as it was hot. "But there's no wind."

Tillit leaned toward me and winked. "Not yet."

Darda grasped my arm and tugged on me. "We should move back. These are very reckless races."

"Only if you don't trust the drivers," Tillit argued.

Darda glared at him. "I trust Xander's skills, but I know nothing of this young man."

Tillit glanced at the young lad and smiled. "You don't need to worry about that young lady. His dad taught him everything he knew, and a little more."

Half the men grasped either side of Xander's raft and the others took hold of Sinbad's vessel. They slid the rafts forward and to a mark in the sand set by one of the men. The tow-men stepped back. A lone man climbed to the top of the tallest sail. In his hand was a straight horn some two feet long.

The pair of sailors stared ahead. All was silent. Everyone watched the limp sails.

I looked around. "So what are we-"

"Shh," Spiros whispered.

I frowned and opened my mouth for a smart-alack reply, but a soft rumble caught my attention. I looked to our left at the rear of the fleet of ships. My eyes widened as I beheld a wall of sand and dust some fifty feet tall coming at us at a quick hadab trot.

CHAPTER 5

My instincts told me to flee. I stepped right, but Darda held tight to me. "There is no need to worry, Miriam," she whispered.

I whipped my head to her smiling face. "Are you nuts? That thing's going to kill us!"

Her eyes twinkled as she smiled at me. "Hold against the storm and see."

I stiffened my jaw and the rest of my body as the storm came charging at us. The sands beneath our feet rolled to our right. A soft flapping arose from the ships as the sails bent against the demand of the coming winds. The sails on the rafts of the two contestants were too tight to flap.

Spiros pulled out some handkerchiefs and handed them to us. "Cover your faces against the dust."

DESERTS OF THE DRAGONS

I took a handkerchief and noticed the work men drape their own handkerchiefs over their faces. I did the same and was surprised to find I could see through the thin fabric, but no dust slipped inside.

As the storm grew closer the man atop the sail lifted his horn. The wind picked up. My own hair beat at my face. Darda kept a firm grasp on me. The stormy sand clouds were only a hundred feet away. Seventy-five. The wind clawed at our clothes.

The man on the sail took a deep breath and blew. A long, mid-range blast of sound echoed from the bell. There was a melodious tune to the horn that made me want to smile, especially when I saw its effects.

The dust cloud turned and drew away from us. Something caught my eyes. I squinted into the orange darkness. Shadows of tall, slim four-legged creatures flickered in the dust. Then they were gone.

So were Xander and Sinbad. At the sound of the horn both competitors stood and opened their sails. The harsh wind filled them and pulled them across the sand at a speed that exceeded that of my wild hadab.

At a hundred feet down the line the dragon men drew out their wings. Sinbad tilted his wings before his full sails. The cloth flapped and turned, and so did the raft. He turned a sharp left away from us and cut across in front of Xander's raft. Their poles brushed against each other. Xander pulled back on his ropes and slowed down to avoid a collision.

Darda gasped and covered her mouth. She whipped her head to Tillit and glared at him. "You were saying?"

He grinned and held up his hands. "Don't take my head until something bad actually happens."

A cheer arose from the men, and I turned back to the race. Sinbad was well ahead of the corner back in our direction. Xander with his wide, less flexible wings had taken the corner wide and now trailed Sinbad by twenty feet. The pair both drew into the stretched some two hundred feet in front of us and flew along at break-neck speed with their sails full of wind.

I frowned and looked around at my small group. No wind disturbed our hair, or even mussed Darda's cloak. "How are they still moving?" I asked my friends.

"It is the power of the sand storm that pulls them along," Spiros told me as he nodded at the open sails of the competitors. "They could travel at that speed all day if the need demanded."

I pointed in the direction of the disappearing dust storm. "But the storm went that way."

"You think a normal dust cloud would turn at the sound of a horn?" Tillit spoke up as he jerked his thumb over his shoulder at the dust cloud. "There's magic in that cloud that makes it stick to the sails. You could get a wet sock and fill it with that wind, and it would fly until you pulled it inside-out."

A cheer from the group of men caught our attention and we looked back to the race. Sinbad had turned against, this time toward us. Xander was forty feet behind them when they both reached the straightaway. Sinbad's men cheered and hollered as he opened his sails and waved at them. The young man leaned back with the ropes in his hands and glanced over his shoulder. Even from that distance I could see his smirk.

I clasped my hands and bit my lower lip as I watched Xander pull up the rear. "Come on! Come on!"

DESERTS OF THE DRAGONS

A heavy hand fell on my shoulder. I looked up into the smiling face of Spiros. His eyes lay on Xander. "Faith, Miriam. Watch and learn why they called him Rabi Rih, Lord of the Wind."

I looked back to Xander. He stood tall and spread his wings wide on either side of him. His wings curved in front of him so that the tips nearly touched either side of the sail.

Xander drew them back and, in the same smooth motion, thrust them forward. A great flap of wind pushed against the sail. The sheet bulged outward and pulled the ropes tight so that Xander grimaced before he leaned back with the ropes clutched tightly in both hands. The miraj slid across the sand in a burst of speed and cut the distance between the rafts by a quarter.

A smile slipped onto my face as Xander drew his wings back and against thrust more speed into the sail. He was now only twenty feet from his opponent.

I stepped forward and cupped my hands over my mouth. "Come on, Xander! Get him!"

Spiros stepped up beside me and cupped a hand over his mouth. "Win the race or I shall have the hand of your Maiden!"

I whipped my head to him. "*What?*" He smiled and winked at me before I noticed the teasing look in his eyes.

"Captain!" Darda scolded him.

Whether serious or not, Xander leaned back so he was at a steep angle and flapped his wings three successive times. The miraj flew forward and passed Sinbad. We onlookers back to allow them to pass between us and the still rafts. They did, and Xander was in the lead across the finish line.

I stumbled through the sand over to his miraj as he released the ropes. The sail fell flat and the wind escaped to dance into the air a brief moment before it disappeared. I leapt at him and wrapped my arms around his neck so I hung there. He gingerly put his arms around me and smiled into my beaming face.

"It looks like you're stuck with me," I teased.

He pecked a kiss on my lips before he lowered me to the ground. "I would have it no other way."

"An impressive display, My Lord," Spiros spoke up as he and the others came up behind me.

Xander looked past me and at his captain. "That is a poor compliment coming from one who dared gamble with my Maiden."

Spiros smiled and bowed his head. "Merely some incentive, My Lord."

"I did not catch what you were to lose should I win."

The captain shook his head. "I am afraid I have no Maiden to gamble with, My Lord, so you must make do with my congratulations on such a close race."

Xander nodded. "Yes, it was very close. Any shorter a distance and I might not have won."

I hit him on the arm and glared at him. "So if you could use your wings the whole time why didn't you do that at the beginning?"

Xander opened his palms in front of him for us to see. "There are painful consequences."

My eyes widened as I beheld the raw and bleeding state of his hands. The skin had been cut open by the rough rope and clumps of drying blood dotted his flesh.

Spiros frowned. "Those cuts are quite deep."

Xander glanced over his shoulder at Sinbad who was surrounded by his men. A small smile teased Xander's lips. "I had little choice. The young man is quite good."

DESERTS OF THE DRAGONS

I cupped his hands in mine and looked over the deep cuts. "We need to get a doctor to look at this."

Xander shook his head. "I need only a salve, some bandages, and a few days of rest."

Sinbad pushed through his men and walked over to us. His eyes were hard and his lips were pursed tightly together, but he stopped before us and bowed his head to Xander. "You have proven your reputation, dragon lord."

Xander set his hand on Sinbad's shoulder. The young man looked up with a questioning gaze. "I wish for you to call me Xander, and were it not for the long course I would be congratulating you."

Sinbad straightened and grinned. "Then I shall be sure to test your words on a shorter course in the races."

Xander shook his head. "It is not my intention to participate in the races, but I shall pray for your success to both goddess and cheer you from the stands."

Sinbad held out his hand. "Then another time, Xander."

My dragon lord shook his hand. "Another time, young Sinbad."

CHAPTER 6

We climbed onto our impatient hadab and continued on our way. I sidled up to Xander who's hands were now bandaged. "So is that what they do out here for sport? Race rafts on sand?"

Xander nodded. "Yes. It is an ancient sport and also a rite of passage for many of their men."

"So how was that race supposed to end Tillit's story?" I asked him.

Tillit trotted up beside me, and glanced past me and at Xander. "I believe I shall finish this story, My Lord."

Xander smiled and bowed his head. "As you wish."

Tillit readjusted himself in his saddle and cleared his throat. "As I was saying, one of the men inside the city was a sailor in his youth, so he devised a plan. Most of the fire was already burnt for cooking, but he got just enough to make a small raft. The wealthy women of the city donated what was left of their extra dresses for a simple sail-"

"And that's how the first sailing raft thingy was made," I finished for him.

He wrinkled his nose. "They're called miraj, My Lady, but yes, that was the first one. The residents strapped the most precious books onto the raft and the sheikh himself had his own naqia brought out to supply the wind."

"What's a naqia?" I wondered.

"Did you see the shadows in that dust storm?" he returned. I nodded. "Those are naqia. They create the wind and the dust storm to protect themselves as they travel from oasis to oasis. But as I was saying, the soldiers at the main gate readied themselves. Archers hid behind the rampart walls ready with their arrows to distract the invading army."

I arched an eyebrow. "He was going to go out the main gate?"

Tillit smiled and pressed a finger to his lips. "Be as patient as the city, My Lady. They waited until dusk when the sun would blind their foes. Then the sheikh gave the signal. The naqia created a great gust of wind that enveloped the whole of the city in a dust storm. The invaders watched in horror as the dust spilled over the walls. They'd never seen anything like a city being swallowed by a dust storm from the inside. That storm was the signal for the archers. They jumped to their feet and shot at anything that moved. It was chaos in the dragon lord camp. That's when the main gates were opened." He looked up into the sky and swept his arm across his front. "The raft flew out the gates and into the main camp of the enemy. Their foes thought they saw an image of magic, a false picture."

"And that's how the raft got it's name," I guessed.

He smiled and nodded. "Yep. The first miraj sailed past them and into the desert, never to be seen again. The dust storm subsided and the city surrendered, but they had still won. When the priests entered the library they found all of the volumes were gone. What hadn't been taken by the sailor was hidden in the city so the invaders wouldn't set fire to it. Doing so would have destroyed those stowed books." He leaned toward me and winked. "To this day they still find a few loose books in hidden cupboards."

"But what about the rest of the books and the guy on the raft?" I asked him.

He straightened and shook his head. "Alas, My Lady, I nor any other storyteller know what happened to him. He disappeared into the desert on the wings of the storm and was never seen again, nor were any of the books ever found."

I slumped in my saddle and frowned. "That's not that great an ending."

"Not all of history is as neat as a story, Miriam," Darda scolded me.

Xander studied me with a teasing smile on his lips. "Perhaps one day the books will be found, but our purpose for coming here lies elsewhere."

I straightened and sighed as I gazed out on the endless desert. "You really think Apuleius can help us?"

Xander followed my gaze into the distance. "We shall see."

I drew my lower lip out and glared at him. "Do you have to be so moody? Couldn't you have just said 'we'll definitely get the answers you want!'?"

He tilted his head toward me and smiled. "We will definitely find the answers you seek."

DESERTS OF THE DRAGONS

I sat up straight and nodded. "There. Not quite my accent, but that's the spirit I want to hear. Now let's get going!"

I made the mistake of clacking my heels against the sides of the hadab. The beast shot off down the desert. I clung to its neck and shut my eyes. My 'friends' were so concerned they laughed before they followed me.

We trod across the desert toward our goal, but night threatened to fall before I glimpsed a clump of shadows far in the distance. I nodded at the shapes. "Please tell me that's where we're going to stay."

Xander smiled. "That is where we will stay for the night."

Tillit trotted up beside me and leaned over to give a wink. "I think you'll like Wahat Alrraei."

I arched an eyebrow. "The what?"

"Wahat Alrraei. It means Oasis of the Shepherd," he told me as he waved a hand at the shadows ahead of us. "You won't see the likes of that place in any fancy city."

"Or a reputable one," Spiros spoke up with a sly smile.

Tillit coughed into his hand. "Perhaps, but I can guarantee that it will be a memorable night."

Xander glanced at Spiros with his lips tightly pursed. "We had best be on our guard."

Spiros's good humor slipped from his face. "You mean the warning of something amiss from Tajir?"

My dragon lord nodded. "Yes. The traders of the desert do not pass along unfavorable rumors that would hurt business unless there is some truth to them."

Tillit glanced between the men with a sly smile on his face. "You gentlemen believe the Red Dragons are up to no good, eh?"

Xander stared ahead of us with his brow furrowed. The shadows came closer and I could make out tall, lush trees. "From the far north to the east we have fought against their plans. I would not be surprised to find them among the traders of the south."

"Any idea what they might be up to?" he persisted.

"What are the aims of faithless dragons but to be faithless dragons?" Xander philosophized. He gripped his reins hard enough to whiten his knuckles as his eyes narrowed. "But whatever their purpose, I will stop them."

I leaned over and set my hand atop his. He looked at me and I smiled back at him. "*We* will stop them."

He returned my smile with one of his own. "

"'We' would also like to reach the oasis before nightfall," Spiros spoke up. He kicked the sides of his beast with his heels and spurred ahead of us before he glanced over his shoulder. There was a sly smile on his lips. "If my slow friends prefer to remain in the desert all night I will go ahead and partake of the entertainment in your place."

Xander chuckled as he glanced at me. "Shall we?"

I grinned and nodded. "Let's do this."

"Xander! Miriam!" Darda scolded us.

"It is merely a race, Darda. Nothing worse than that," Tillit replied.

She glared at him. "What will the sheikh say of such an entrance?"

Spiros laughed and kicked his hadab so the beast sped forward. "That we are late!"

CHAPTER 7

Our group sped along the desert, and even Darda was not to be left behind. The large trees of the oasis stretched into sky as we grew nearer, and I could see that they surrounded a wide pool. Thin grass speckled the ground around the edges of the water and beneath the cool shade of the trees. A large corral stood off to the far left and contained some hundred hadab that chewed away at dry grass.

The green area was a quarter of a mile wide and long, and at that moment was crowded with people and tents. The tents were made of canvas and stood taller than me. They were propped up with poles and the flaps on the front were open to show off their spacious interiors. Carpets covered the ground and several of the tents had mounds of pillows in their corners.

We slowed down as a cool breeze wafted over us. The scents of grass and campfire wafted into my nostrils. I could see the flickering flames of a large fire rise up from the center of the many tents.

"Alzalam makes good money this year," Tillit commented.

Spiros glanced at Xander. "The rumors seem not to have harmed his business."

Xander nodded. "So it would seem. We shall see if there are any accommodations to be had."

We trotted into the outskirts of the camp where we were stopped by a tanned man in white robes. The stranger was about forty, of mid-height and with a slim physique. He bowed his head to us. "Allow me to take your animals, Lord Xander."

Xander dismounted and handed the reins to the man. "It has been a long time, Alththania."

The man smiled at Xander. "It is an honor to be remembered by such a dragon as yourself, Your Lordship."

"Alzalam has one of the best servants in the whole of the desert," Xander complimented the man. He looked past the retainer at the tents and nodded in their direction. "Is your master among his guests?"

Alththania nodded. "He is, Your Lordship."

My dragon lord turned to us. "Let us go see our host."

We dismounted and handed the reins to the servant. As I handed mine off to him, he studied me with a careful eye before he turned to Darda. I followed Xander through the maze of tents to the brightly lit center. A great fire surrounded by stones cast its orange glow on the canvases. The fuel was a strange round wood that let off a sweet odor like lilacs.

DESERTS OF THE DRAGONS

Dozens of people sat on logs around the fire. Their chatter was a welcomed change from the quiet of the desert. A man in a flowing white robe walked among them, stopping and talking to the many groups. His appearance was that of a man of sixty about my height and with a little too much belly bump beneath the robes. He sported a white beard and long hair that bounced on his shoulders. His black bushy eyebrows stood out even against his tanned skin.

He lifted his dark eyes as we entered the area and they widened. A wide grin stretched across his face as he hurried over to us and opened his arms. "Your Lordship! Welcome! Welcome!" He embraced Xander in a tight hug before he pulled them to arm's length and looked him over. "It has been the life of a hadab since we last met!"

Xander smiled. "A very great time indeed, old friend."

Alzalam draped his arm over Xander's back and led him toward the fire. "Have you come to enjoy the Jame and-ahem-" he gave a wink, "-the lovely priestesses?"

I frowned and coughed into my hand. Alzalam looked over his shoulder at me. A sly smile slid onto his lips as his eyes flickered to Xander. "You must excuse me, Your Lordship. You seem to have found quite the servant, though I must admit her clothes are rather unusual. Where is she from?"

"She is my Maiden from the other world," Xander explained.

Alzalam stopped and winced before he turned to me with a flourishing bow. "My apologies, Your Ladyship. It was meant as a joke."

"I'll gladly take up your offer to Lord Xander," Tillit spoke up.

Alzalam set his eyes on Tillit and grinned. "Tillit, you old swine! Has a cold bed brought you to the hot desert? And Spiros! I have heard someone was foolish enough to make you captain of the guard for the great city of Alexandria."

"Someone very foolish," Spiros agreed as he shook the sheikh's hand.

Alzalam backed up and gestured to me. "Forgive me for not noticing all of you, my friends, but the beauty of His Lordship's Maiden blinded me to your presence."

Spiros smiled. "A very smooth save, Alzalam, but tell me, does my record still stand?"

Alzalam laughed and nodded. "It does, my friend, but you have a challenger this night. I believe he is a man from my nephew's party. He means to win your record for himself."

I glanced at Darda who stood by my side. "What record?"

She shook her head. "What they elude to was far before my time, Miriam."

Alzalam overheard us and pretended to be aghast. His eyes widened and he whipped his head to Spiros who stood at his side. "Have you not told them of your prowess with the flute?"

I snorted. "The flute?"

Alzalam slipped over to me and shook his head. "Ah, but Your Ladyship does not know the flutes of the desert. Made as they are from our few trees, their sound radiates off the desert like the heat, but the sound is cool to the ears. One need only blow-" he mimicked the act of blowing into a flute, "-and one might even call forth the naqia to listen to their sweet song."

DESERTS OF THE DRAGONS

I arched an eyebrow. "So what do these naqia look like?"

He winked at me. "You shall see. I am sure my old friend Spiros here shall not disappoint the crowd by refusing the challenger."

Spiros smiled and bowed his head. "I will gladly accept the challenge."

Alzalam laughed and clapped him on the back. "That is the spirit of the Jame!" He raised his arms and clapped into the air. The dozens of people around us quieted their conversations and turned to our host. "Attention, my worthy friends! Tonight I have a rare treat for you! A contest of skill between two honorable challengers for the sake of honor, entertainment-"

"Out with it, Father, before our guests grow old!" a young voice called from the crowd. Laughter arose from the onlookers.

Alzalam smiled as he wagged his finger at a young man. The stranger wore a white robe like our host, but his face was clean-shaven and his eyes were darker. "You must be patient, my son. What I propose is a flute contest to see who may bring forth one of the beautiful naqia!"

The crowd was all chattering as the man walked up to our group and stood beside Alzalam. "Patience can be an expensive virtue, Father, but you must introduce me to our new guests. I do not believe I know them."

Alzalam set a hand on the young man's shoulder and swept his other hand over us. "These are many old friends, and some new ones. My guests, this is my son, Tifl."

The young man smiled as he shook the hands of the men. "You must pardon the name, my friends. I have only my father to blame."

"Are you not my child?" Alzalam countered.

"I am, dear Father, but-" Tifl reached me and paused as he studied me with his dark eyes. "My Father, who is this creature of loveliness?"

"She is my Maiden, and her name is Miriam," Xander spoke up.

Tifl grasped my hand and planted a gentle kiss on the back. A smile curled onto his lips as his eyes flickered up to me. "You are as beautiful as a cool well after a long journey across the desert, Miriam."

"Sounds-um, refreshing," I commented.

His gaze caught mine and I noticed a slyness at the corner of his lips. "You have no idea, my dear Miriam."

I could sense Xander's attentive eyes on me. So did Alzalam. Our host hurried forward and extracted my hand from that of his son. "See if your cousin has arrived with Spiros's challenger, my son."

Tifl bowed his head. "As you wish, Father." He disappeared into the growing darkness that surrounded the camp.

Alzalam followed him with his eyes until he was out of sight and turned back to us with a soft smile. "You must forgive him, my friends. He is young and beauty excites him."

Xander shook his head. "There is nothing to apologize for, though we would ask you a favor."

Alzalam bowed his head. "Anything, Your Lordship."

"What do you know of these rumors of danger in the desert?"

Alzalam raised his head and pursed his lips. "You refer to the small suns, do you not?" Xander nodded. Our host sighed and shook his head. "I cannot give you any answers, my friend, because I do not have any for myself. I myself have not seen the lights but others have, though when I have sent my son to look he has come back to say he saw nothing."

"Did he go as far as the Nasi Cliffs?" Tillit wondered.

Alzalam shook his head. "No. I would not allow him to desecrate that tomb with mere curiosity."

"What are the Nasi Cliffs?" I spoke up.

Alzalam turned to me with soft eyes, but no smile. "They are the ancient home of the humans who once ruled the desert. The humans carved their homes from the cliffs and grew their food on the plateau above their dwellings, but that was many thousands of years ago. The cliffs are now abandoned, and some say they are haunted by the spirits of those humans who lived and died there so long ago."

"What do you say, our worthy host?" Spiros asked him.

Alzalam glanced at him out of the corner of his eyes. "I say I will not break the sanctity of such a dwelling, and will leave others who are not of my tribe to dare break the peace that resides in those quiet tombs of time."

Xander set a hand on Alzalam's shoulder and smiled down at our host. "Let us celebrate their memory and the Jame by a toast. How is the beer this year? And the wine?"

Alzalam grinned and wrapped his arm around Xander's back to lead him toward the fire. "The beer is so fine that you will think it ambrosia, and the wine is as sweet as honey. But do not take my word for it. Alththania!"

Alththania appeared from the crowd of people and bowed before his master. "Yes, sir?"

"Bring out the kegs! Roll out the barrels! There shall be drinks for all!"

CHAPTER 8

A loud cheer rang from the crowd and the drinks were carried out on the shoulders of many servants. The barrels of wine were carefully rolled out and set upright where their tops were opened. Mugs were dipped into the kegs and barrels, and passed out to the revelers who occupied the camp.

"Is it not customary for the son to fetch the drink?" Tillit asked Alzalam as he was handed a mug.

Alzalam sighed and shook his head. "Alas, but my young son cannot perform his duties. He is afflicted with the Rash."

"The what?" I spoke up.

"He is allergic to the desert berries, and any contact in any form will cause him to develop rashes on his skin," Xander explained to me.

DESERTS OF THE DRAGONS

Alzalam nodded. "Yes, but do not take his absence as an insult. He will return when the drink is gone, so I ask that you do your part to allow my son to come back."

Tillit raised his mug and grinned. "I will do that, our worthy host!"

Our group took a seat on one of the logs near the fire. Xander sat down beside me and handed me a mug brimming with sweet-smelling wine. "I dare say the wine of the desert berries rivals even those of the vineyards of Alexandria."

I took a sip and smacked my lips as the sweet wine tingled them. "Tastes like melted candy."

Tillit held out his mug to me. "Then perhaps Your Ladyship would like to try the beer." There was a sly smile on his lips I didn't like.

I leaned forward and sniffed the beer. The scent tickled my nose with its heavy odor. I reared back and wrinkled my nose. "What's in it?"

Tillit chuckled. "Only the finest wild grass the oasis have to offer flavored with the delicate milk of the hadab."

I cringed. "I think I'll stick with wine."

"You have opened the casks without me, Uncle?" a voice called from the darkness around the fire.

From the shadows came forth Sinbad, and behind him walked his crew. Many of the oasis guests gasped and leapt to their feet. Some of the men pulled their female companions behind them and glared at the rough-looking newcomers.

Alzalam stood and held up his hands. "It is all right, my friends! They will do you no harm." He walked over and slipped his arm over Sinbad's shoulders as he looked grinning at the young sailor. "He is merely my nephew, the child of my only sister."

"You began the festivities early, my uncle," Sinbad commented.

Alzalam gestured to us. "My eminent guests inquired of this year's drink and I did not wish to disappoint them. Allow me to introduce you to them."

Sinbad's eyes fell on us and he smirked. "They had the pleasure of meeting my men and me earlier, Uncle."

Xander smiled and bowed his head. "Likewise."

Alzalam clapped his hands. "Excellent! Excellent! But I have better news, Nephew. This gentleman-" he gestured to Spiros, "-has accepted a challenge from your man. Why do you not call him forth to entertain my guests?"

Sinbad studied Spiros with a frown. "Very well, Uncle, but I do not believe he will provide much sport for my man."

Our host laughed and clapped Sinbad's back. "We shall see, Nephew! Or rather, hear!" He spun around to face the fire and the other guests where he raised his hands in the air. "Friends! Companions! We shall have good sport tonight! A flute contest!"

A murmur arose from the crowd as Sinbad glanced over his shoulder. One of the crew stepped forward to stand beside Sinbad. It was the same man who had blown the trumpet to frighten away the sandstorm. He bowed to Alzalam before he straightened and studied Spiros with a steady gaze.

Sinbad clapped his hand on the man's shoulders and grinned at us. "This is my champion. His name is Wahid Samat, the Silent One, for since birth he has been unable to speak. That curse has given him the gift of much breath, and with that he tames the sandstorms and wins any flute contest."

DESERTS OF THE DRAGONS

"Everyone take your seats! We shall begin at once!" Alzalam called out.

The gatherers seated themselves around the fire. Its flickering light cast long shadows across the ground as the calm of night descended on us. Spiros and Wahid were seated on a log to themselves and handed long, narrow flutes. The wood was smooth and the tiny holes in the top were set close together.

Spiros smiled at his rival. "You may be first, if you please."

Wahid nodded and lifted his flute to his mouth. He blew, and an enchanting tune slipped from the mouth of the wood instrument. The music sang like a folk song in time with his fingers as they danced up and down flute. More than one guest climbed to their feet and spun around in a circle before the crackling fire. The whole of Sinbad's company clapped in time with the flute, but they couldn't drown out the sound of the quick ditty.

The music lingered in the air even as the man lowered the pipe. The audience clapped and Alzalam stood and clapped loudest. "Wonderful! Just wonderful! Now quiet! Quiet, everyone, and let us listen!"

The camp quieted. I looked around. Many of those present looked around us as though searching for something.

I leaned close to Xander and lowered my voice to a whisper. "What are we waiting for?"

"If the flute player's skill is fine and his music sincere then tradition tells that a naqia will come and bless him and his company," Xander explained.

My eyes widened and I straightened to look around. Nothing stirred save for the occasional shift of the audience.

Alzalam lowered his arm and smiled at Wahid "Never mind. You played admirably, and I am sure some day you will be blessed by the naqia. I only hope I am in your company to hear that beautiful sound when it is played."

Tillit raised his mug in the air. "And to reap the blessings of a good harvest of desert berries."

Alththania handed Alzalam a mug and our host raised the glass in the air. "I will drink to-"

"A moment, if you would, dear uncle," Sinbad spoke up. He stepped before the seated Spiros and frowned down upon him. "We shall drink the blessing of both of them, but only after this dragon plays."

Spiros smiled and bowed his head. "As you wish."

The mugs were lowered and a hush fell over the crowd as Spiros raised the flute to his lips. He closed his eyes, took a deep breath and blew.

I never paid much attention to music, but even my novice self could tell this was something completely different. The haunting melody that emanated from the flute gently swayed the air with its vibrations so that one didn't so much hear the music as *feel* the song.

Spiros sat as still as a majestic oak, but his hands were different. His fingers were as nimble as deer as they slipped up and down the flute. The music flowed from beneath those fingers as though he crafted each tune from the air itself.

No one swayed in time to the tune. No once danced. We didn't have to. It was enough to sit and listen to the flow of that sweet melody.

We were hardly aware when his fingers stopped their dance and he opened his eyes. Spiros lowered the flute and turned his head to the left without moving the rest of the body.

My eyes widened as a pure-white creature stepped out of the darkness. It was a unicorn.

The horse-like creature had a single, spiraled horn that protruded two feet from its forehead. Its white mane lay against its smooth, muscular body, and its tail swung in time with its trot. The majestic beast's short hair shimmered in the firelight and its perfect hooves made not a sound on the sand. Its wide, crystal-blue eyes held a steady gaze on Spiros as it walked toward him. The creature stopped five feet from the log and bowed its head.

Spiros smiled and returned the gesture. The beast turned away and returned back into the darkness.

There was a long silence before Alzalam's soft voice broke the quiet. "By all the goddesses, what a beautiful creature." He shook himself and turned to Spiros with a smile. "And you have given us that rare treat, my friend! Let us drink to that indeed!"

He raised his mug and the stupor that lay over the whole company was broken. We all raised our mugs and gave a cheer before downing the contents.

I took a swig and turned to Xander. "So that was a naqia?"

He glanced at where the creature had gone and nodded. "Yes. I have not seen one for a great while, but their beauty is always breathtaking."

"So why didn't you just tell me that the naqia was a unicorn?"

He turned to me and smiled. "Because that is not what they are called in our world."

Spiros walked over to us and took a seat between Xander and Tillit. The sus raised his mug to the flutist. "A fine performance, my boy. Even better than the last time I heard you play. I dare say you attracted a leader of some naqia herd that time."

Spiros lifted the flute to study its smooth design. "I have this to thank. I have never seen a better one."

"And it is yours, my friend!" Alzalam called out as he strode up to us. His eyes twinkled with fun as he winked at Spiros. "A gift of song for a gift of blessing, and I will not take 'no' for an answer."

Spiros smiled and bowed his head. "I thank you for the honor, sir."

Alzalam turned toward the fire and raised his arms above his head. "Now let us drink and be merry, for tomorrow the Jame begins!"

CHAPTER 9

The night was long and the drink flowed like small waterfalls into the gullets of many present at the camp. I myself watched with a mixture of fascination and disgust as barrel after barrel fell before the thirst of the the revelers, my own dragon lord among them.

Darda and I sat on a log at the edge of the fire light. Clasped in our hands were two untouched mugs of the fine wine. Before us danced many of the drunken celebrators, most of them very badly. They stumbled over their own feet and that of the others as they went around and around the bonfire. Xander and Spiros were a part of the bunch, and no less steady on their feet as the others.

Tillit plopped himself down on the log beside Darda. There was a mug in one hand and a smile on his face. His cheeks were flushed as he leaned toward Darda. "Didn't I tell you you'd have fun?"

She leaned away from him and sneered. "I fail to see the 'fun' in such foolish behavior."

He hiccuped and sat straight. "That's because you don't know what it means. Here, I'll show you." He stumbled to his feet and grabbed her hand.

Darda yelped as she was dragged off the log. Tillit tripped over his own feet, and together they were pulled by gravity onto the soft sand. Mugs went flying and limbs were tangled together as they thrashed on the ground.

Tillit raised his head and blinked. "What happened?"

"You fell, you oaf, and took me with you!" Darda snarled.

He grinned. "Did I?"

Darda shoved him away. "Get off me!"

"I would, but I-*hiccup*-can't seem to get up," he replied.

The pair pulled and yanked, but they were stuck together. I set my mug in the sand at my feet and stood. "I think I'll let you two play this out alone while I go to the bathroom."

Darda tried to free herself, but Tillit's legs caught hers. "You should not go alone, Miriam!"

I didn't turn around as I gave a wave over my shoulder. "I'll stay in the oasis and be back in a minute."

I wandered away from the firelight and into the darkness beyond the tents. Small bushes and the tall palm trees cast darker shadows behind them and offered a place for privacy for me to relieve myself. I stepped up to a particularly large bush and was assessing its usability when something beyond the shrub caught my attention.

DESERTS OF THE DRAGONS

Over the top of the bush I spotted a strange light. It appeared four feet off the ground, but it wasn't the glow of a torch. The light was too consistent. It swung back and forth like a lantern, but there was no flicker of a candle or burning oil. It almost looked like-

"A flashlight?" I whispered.

My muffled words made the light pause, and I caught a glimpse of a beam on the sandy ground. There was a soft click and the beam vanished. I heard footsteps hurry away from me. I moved to follow it, but a hand grabbed my arm.

I yelped as I was spun around. Xander's shadow-cloaked face looked into mine. There was no hint of intoxication as he spoke. "You have been gone far too long."

I arched an eyebrow. "Have you been pretending to be drunk?"

"Perhaps," he commented as he looked over my head in the direction I'd been looking. "What caught your attention so thoroughly?"

I looked back at the spot over the bush. "I thought I saw something like a flashlight over there."

"A 'flashlight?'" he repeated.

I nodded. "Yeah, it's something from my old world that uses electricity to shine a light. Kind of like a lantern, but without oil."

Xander grasped my hand and guided me around the bush. "Let us see what we might find."

Together we strode over to the spot where I'd seen the light. I nodded at our feet. "I think the light was here."

He stooped and scanned the ground before he shook his head. "There are too many footprints to follow a single one." He stood and turned to me. "You are sure of what you saw?"

I frowned. "Of course I'm sure. Why wouldn't I be?"

He glanced around at the deep darkness. "Because such technology should not exist in this world. It is forbidden to bring any such items through the Portal."

I crossed my arms over my chest and narrowed my eyes. "I know what I saw."

Xander pursed his lips as he grasped my upper arms. "Then we must keep our eyes open for more lights, but let us return. The others may be worried."

The revelry continued long through the night, but Xander and I retired. We slept in one of the pillow-filled tents, and in the morning I woke up with rumpled hair and a slight touch of hangover. I sat up and groaned as my head swam.

Xander rolled over beside me on the clump of pillows and wrapped his arms around my waist. He buried his head into my side and smiled. "You smell of the desert."

I snorted. "So like fermented desert berries?"

He nuzzled me. His soft words trembled against my side. "You smell of the sweet desert grass mixed with the cool breeze across the hot sands."

I raised an arm and sniffed myself. The scent made me wrinkle my nose before I looked down at him. "Are we smelling the same me?"

He drew me down onto the pillows and leaned above me. A devilish smile slipped onto his lips. "I would like to do more than smell you." A soft scratch against the front flap of our tent caught our attention. Xander's shoulders drooped, but he looked over his shoulder at the entrance. "Yes?"

Spiros's voice floated through the flap. "We must leave soon, My Lord, or we will not make the city before the heat."

Xander frowned. "Prepare the hadab. We will be out in a short while."

There was a ring of bemusement in Spiros's reply. "They are already prepared."

My dragon lord sighed and lifted himself off me. "Very well. We will be out directly."

"Very good, My Lord." His footsteps retreated from the flap.

Xander sat beside me and ran a hand through his hair as he shook his head. "He takes great pleasure in vexing me."

I sat up and patted him on the shoulder. "Friends are like that."

He glanced over his shoulder at me. "You have felt the same?"

I nodded. "Oh yeah. There's this one friend back where I came from who was real pushy. She's kind of the reason I got here, too."

Xander smiled. "Then I will thank her in my prayers once we reach the Temple. Let us prepare."

We exited the tent a short while later and found the small village alive with activity. Packed hadab waited beside tents as servants and masters prepared for the final leg of the journey. The classy clientele of the oasis were assisted onto their animals and sat atop the hadab's like sacks of flour.

Spiros stood nearby watching the scene, and we joined him at his side. He glanced to his right at Xander. His lips were pursed tightly. "We may have trouble with this group."

Xander arched an eyebrow. "Why?"

Spiros nodded at the sacks of flour and their heavy-laden hadabs. "They are inexperienced with their animals, and many of them brought enough gold to attract every bandit in the desert."

I leaned forward to look across Xander at Spiros. "But isn't this supposed to be some sort of a holy trip or something? People aren't supposed to attack people right now, right?"

"Greed would rob its own grandmother, and the bandits of the desert are followers of such a principal," Spiros told me.

"Then we will help speed them along as well as we might," Xander commented.

"My friends!" the jolly voice of Alzalam called to us. He came over from the packing with a smile on his face. "Did you sleep well?"

Xander bowed his head. "Yes, we thank you. The renowned comfort of your tents still holds true."

"Excellent! And now you shall be off with the others to finish the Jame. I hope you like our ancient city," he mused.

"Even though it is filled with the symbols of its ancient capture," a voice spoke up. We turned to see Tifl come our way and he joined us with a smile on his face. "Still, there is much pride among its people."

Alzalam frowned at his son. "It is not polite to insult guests."

Xander held up his hand and shook his head. "It is quite all right, my good host. I would not like to see Alexandria ever occupied by transgressors."

Tifl bowed his head to Xander. "I am glad you agree with me, Your Lordship, especially as I have come to wish you a safe journey."

DESERTS OF THE DRAGONS

"That is a journey we must now commence or the worst of the heat will be upon us before we reach the city," Xander agreed.

Our hadab were brought to us and we mounted the beasts. The others guests were specks on the horizon as we waved to our hosts and left the green land among the white sands.

I glanced at Xander. "So how far is it to the city again?"

"Not more than half a day's ride. If my letter has reached Apuleius I hope that a fine lunch awaits us," he replied.

We traveled across the hot sands for several hours. The other former guests of the oasis, laden as they were by their treasures, were slower and we gained ground on them until they were scarcely fifty yards ahead of us.

The desert stretched out on all sides of us. Nothing stirred save for the occasional dust devil that swept past us. I was ready to ask how far the city was when I caught sight of movement on the horizon.

I leaned forward and squinted. "What's that?"

Xander smiled. "It is the creatures of blessing."

I perked up. "Unicorns?"

He nodded as he pulled his animal to the left. "Yes, but they will not grant a blessing to us as we are."

"What do you mean by that?" I asked my dragon lord as we followed him to the left. The group ahead of us also steered leftward.

"The naqia travel from oasis to oasis within the safety of their self-made sandstorm," Xander explained as we stopped some fifty yards from where we pulled off. We turned to face the oncoming sandstorm. The wall of dust was twice the size as the one that had pushed the sails in the race. "Though they are beasts of virtue, they are not beneath stampeding over anything that stands in the way of their travels."

"So they'd squish anything that they ran over?" I guessed.

"Precisely."

I looked back to the sandstorm and frowned. "Not very nice, are they?"

"It is a matter of survival," Spiros spoke up. "Rare creatures attract poachers, and poachers will not hesitate to harm the beasts."

I snorted and pointed at the sandstorm that came within a hundred yards of us. "How are they going to harm anything in that storm?"

"They must stop for water at some point, and it is at that time where they are most vulnerable," Spiros told me.

Darda set her hand on my shoulder and smiled at me. "Are they the less beautiful for their protection?"

I shrugged. "Well, I wouldn't put more than one in a petting zoo."

The sandstorm picked up the dust around us. My hair whipped my face as the hadab beneath me reared back its head and pulled at the reins.

"Whoa there, old-um, thing," I soothed as the creature snorted and pawed at the sand. I glanced at Darda. "What's the matter with this thing? Hasn't it seen a sandstorm before?"

Darda tightened her hold on her own reins as her beast caused the same trouble. "There is something amiss here. They should have no fear of the sandstorm."

My heart skipped a beat as I looked down at the sands. "Maybe it's not the storm they're afraid of."

DESERTS OF THE DRAGONS

Xander looked out on the sandstorm and frowned. "Everyone keep your guard-"

A loud trumpet broke the monotonous roar of the wind. The noise was a signal that called a dozen dark forms that flew out of the top of the sandstorm. They stretched their short wings and glided toward us. The sandstorm passed as they landed with a crunch on the sands between the lead group and our own. The dragons were all men, but they hid their features with loose tan clothing and scarves over the lower half of their faces. They drew curved swords from the sashes around their waists and broke into two groups. One went to the lead group and the other half stalked toward us. The group ahead of ours spurred on their beasts and raced across the desert with the swordsmen close behind them.

Spiros and Xander leapt from their hadabs and drew their swords. Our half of the attackers gave a battle shout and rushed them. The clash of steel against steel rang loudly across the quiet sands. The count was two against six as Xander and Spiros ducked and parried thrust after swing.

Spiros leapt back as one of his opponents made a wild swing across his chest. The blade of the sword sliced open his garb, but not his flesh. He blocked a blow from his other opponent and glanced at Xander. "They mean to kill us!"

"Then we have no choice but to return the privilege!" Xander called back.

The men dragon battled with their swords as Darda and I held back with Tillit beside us. Two of the attackers, one from each group, managed to slip around the men and hurry toward us.

Darda slipped from her hadab and grabbed my leg. She looked up at me and tugged. "Get down, Miriam!"

I shook myself and slid off the saddle just as the pair reached us. One of them gave a cry and swung their sword at us. Darda drew her blades from beneath her heavy garb and blocked the blow. Tillit grabbed the reins of our retreating hadab and placed himself out of harms way.

The other attacker stepped around her and lunged at me. I slipped around to the right side of my startled hadab. The creature brayed and stumbled to the right as the dragon man pushed it forward. I grabbed the swinging reins and pulled the beast back between us. My water bottle hit me in the face, but the knock gave me an idea.

I tore the bottle from my saddle and let go of the reins to open the cap. My hadab took off and left me without any cover. The masked dragon yelled and lifted his sword with both hands over his head to bring it down on mine.

I splashed some of my water on my hands and flung it at his face. The droplets combined to form a whip that lashed one of his cheeks. He spun in a circle and fell face-first into the sand. His sword dropped to the ground a few feet from him.

I grinned and looked at my comrades. I wish I hadn't.

Spiros and Xander dispatched their last foes with swift strokes of their swords across the chests of their attackers. Blood splattered the ground as the men dropped to their knees and fell onto their sides beside the first victims of the dragon men's sword skills.

Darda herself criss-crossed her dagger across the man's throat. He let out a garbled gasp before he, too, dropped to the ground dead. I covered my mouth and tried to tamp down the bile that rose in my throat.

Xander cleaned his sword with sand and turned to me as he sheathed it. His expression was severe as he walked over and grasped my hands. He looked into my eyes. "Are you unharmed?"

I swallowed the puke and nodded. "Y-yeah, but did you have to kill them?"

He pursed his lips. "There was no choice."

Spiros joined us and looked over the bodies. His eyes fell on mine. "One of them appears not to have had that choice." The man groaned.

Xander knelt beside him and rolled the man over. His face was covered in sand. The man's eyes fluttered open and fell on Xander. They widened and he tried to scurry backward, but Xander set his hand on the man's shoulder and pinned him to the sand.

"Why did you attack us?" Xander questioned him.

The man sneered at him. "Why do you think?"

Xander shook his head. "You were not after gold. Any fool could see the but you and your companions purposefully landed behind them so they could have a chance to escape. Why then did you wish for no witnesses to the battle?"

He grinned at us. "Just ask Sinbad." The dragon bit down on one of his sharp teeth. A fine powder of dust flew from his mouth.

Xander grabbed the man's jaw and wrenched it open, but the man's eyes rolled back and his head lolled to one side. His body went limp upon the sand and his chest ceased to move.

Xander dropped the man and sneered at the corpse as he stood. "The coward has killed himself with poison."

Darda shook her head. "There is no honor among thieves."

Tillit stooped and picked up one of the blades. He stood and examined the curved sword. "This is a little strange. This blade's new."

Spiros glanced at the other weapons in the sand. "As are all the others."

"Maybe they robbed somebody else before us," I suggested as Xander took the blade from Tillit.

My dragon lord studied the new weapon and shook his head. "Refined metals are rare in the desert, and so the sand thieves cherish their weapons above all else. They would not all use a new blade unless they were given as gifts."

I arched an eyebrow. "So you're saying someone's sponsoring them?"

Xander slipped the sword between his sword scabbard and waist. "That is a possibility."

"He did mention Sinbad," Spiros reminded us.

Tillit frowned and shook his head. "And I don't believe it. He might be a kid, but he's not that kind of guy."

Xander glanced at the horizon. "We will need to investigate further, but for now we must continue on before night falls or more thieves come."

I nodded at the bodies. "What about them?"

"We will alert the authorities to their location, and if they choose not to retrieve them then the sands will take them."

DESERTS OF THE DRAGONS

CHAPTER 10

We rounded up our hadabs and continued on our journey. An hour later we crested a sand dune some hundred feet high and looked down on a valley. Below us was a large bowl-shaped depression, and in the center stood a walled city of dried mud. The yellow tint of the thirty-foot thick walls was like a beacon in the empty desert. Beyond the walls lay a maze of single-floor houses that were packed tightly together. Narrow streets, placed like an afterthought among the hodgepodge of houses, wound their way through the houses to the center of the city.

In the middle of the metropolis where all roads met there arose an acropolis. The vertical climb rose some two hundred feet above the desert floor and its steep slopes were speckled with rocks and worn brick walls. The buildings scattered along the flat top were made of carved stone rather than sun-baked mud. The grandest of the buildings, the one at the rear farthest from the road up to the hilltop, was a palace of spiraled towers at its four corners and a large archway that led into its confines.

I nodded at the acropolis. "Are the priests compensating for something?"

"That is the High City, the ancient dwelling of the former ruler of the city and their water goddess, Alihat Dhahabia," Xander told me.

I arched an eyebrow. "You think she's still around?"

He shook his head. "I have never heard of anyone meeting her, but we must hurry."

A single narrow gate was the only entrance into the walled city. We traveled down the slope and were a hundred yards from the entrance when a contingent of riders on hadabs passed out of the gate. They galloped in our direction.

Xander stopped us and allowed the riders to meet us some seventy yards from the finish. The men were dressed in white robes that flowed over their saddles. Each clutched a spear in one hand with white tips that glistened in the bright sunlight.

Hoods covered their faces, but the leader drew back their hood and revealed himself to be a young man of twenty-five with tanned skin. He looked us over before his gaze settled on Xander. "You are Lord Xander, are you not?"

Xander nodded. "I am, and you are the guards of the city and its temple. What brought you out beyond the boundaries of the walls?"

The man smiled. "You did, Your Lordship. Those who traveled with you alerted us to an attack, and we were ordered to come to your rescue. I am Captain Benedictus, and these-"

he gestured to the other soldiers who removed their hoods, "- are my men."

My dragon lord chuckled. "You have saddled your beasts for nothing, but you may use them to find the bodies of those who attacked us. They lie a few miles back on the road."

The leader of the guards pursed his lips. "I see. We will investigate this matter at once." He glanced over his shoulder at his men. "Follow me."

The troop galloped in the direction we had come. Spiros looked to Xander. "So it seems we were the targets after all."

Xander nodded. "Yes. Someone did not wish for us to enter the city, and even in its walls we must keep our guard up. Come."

Xander led us across the valley to the gate. The entrance had no doors, but a wrought-iron gate hung from the top of the archway. A single slice of a thick rope would have brought it down and sealed the city inside a nearly-impenetrable defense. The guards in robes who stood on either side of the arch, however, reminded visitors and citizens alike that that defense wasn't nearly impenetrable enough.

We rode into the central square, an open area that looked more like a crooked hexagon than any square I'd ever seen. The corners of houses jutted into its domain, and against every available wall stood a stall. The sellers called out in loud, clear voices advertisements for cheap wares and one-of-a-kind gifts. Hordes of buyers mingled between the stalls. The visitors gaped at the items up for sale. The citizens sneered.

On the left and down a side street stood a long, low building. The scent of hadab excrement wafted over to me, and I saw a few of the animals go inside the wide barn doors that were positioned in the center-side of the building. A few groups of men gathered against the long wall of the hadab stables. They watched us with narrowed eyes.

I shrank in my saddle as more sullen gazes fell on us. "Is this a festival or a funeral?"

"The mood is rather dire," Spiros agreed.

"All the more that we should hurry to the temple to find what is the matter," Xander suggested.

Xander led us through the masses. My attention was caught by one particularly large stall. The front had a table with wound scrolls. Behind the table were four short desks with angled tops. Hunched over the tops were four men in white robes. They each held a quill and wrote on one scroll while they referenced another.

I tugged on his sleeve and nodded at the stall. "What are they doing there?"

"Those are scribes who sell copies of the books in the library," Xander told me.

I frowned and turned to Tillit. "You said they got away with the library."

He nodded. "So they did, but that was a couple thousand years ago. The priests made their own library and now run a tidy business selling what they got."

A weathered face was shoved into mine. "Pretty trinkets for a pretty lady!" he shouted as he held up a deep box piled with jewels. They sparkled in the sunlight. "Won't the pretty lady buy some trinkets to celebrate the Jame?"

Tillit slipped between us and wiggled his fingers as his eyes eagerly looked over the jewels. "My my, what have we here?" He picked up a red jewel as beautiful as any ruby and examined the merchandise. The sus laughed and tossed it back onto the box. "I could make better forgeries sitting in the hull of a ship with only a whittle knife and a block of wood."

The seller tucked the box under his arm and glared at Tillit. "I sell only the best-"

"In terrible fakes," Tillit finished.

"How do you know they're fakes?" I asked him as the seller fumed in front of us.

"Let me show you." Tillit plucked the ruby-like jewel from the box.

"Hey!" the seller yelped as he lunged for the jewel.

Tillit stepped to one side and held out his foot. The man tripped and fell face-first into the dust. The box clattered to the ground face-up beside him.

"You hold the jewel like this-" he held the jewel flat in his palm, "-and do you see the tiny bits of fog inside?"

I leaned forward and nodded. "Yeah. What is it?"

"Glass. Cheap glass, too." He tossed the fake jewel back into the box.

"If your lesson is done-" Darda spoke up a few yards ahead of us. Xander and Spiros were stopped a few feet ahead of her. She glared at Tillit, "-then we must be going."

Tillit offered me his arm and grinned. "Our friends await, My Lady."

I smiled and took his arm. We passed through the market and along the winding road. The path led to the base of the acropolis where we found the road blocked by another pair of robed guards. Close at their backs was a cage occupied by pigeons.

"More guards," Spiros whispered to Xander. My dragon lord nodded, but said nothing.

"And no pilgrims," Tillit added as he glanced over the deserted road. "This place should be packed with people going to the temple."

One of the guards stepped into our path and held up his hand. "Halt!"

We stopped, but Xander stepped forward. "I am Lord Xander of Alexandria, and I demand passage."

The guard looked him over with a derisive sneer on his face. "We were not informed of your coming."

Xander frowned. "I was not aware a lord of the dragons needed to make an appointment to visit the temple. Who told you a warning was needed?"

The guard stood to his full height which fell short of Xander's by half a head. "There's been a lot of trouble lately, but if you are the Lord Xander than you should be able to prove-" Xander slipped forward and, in the same motion, drew Bucephalus from its sheath.

He pressed the blade against the man's throat before the guard could even blink. "Is that proof enough?" Xander asked the guard. The guard swallowed hard and very carefully nodded. Xander stepped back and sheathed his sword. "Now please step aside."

The guard rubbed his neck, but stepped out of our way. We trudged on with our beasts. I glanced over my shoulder. The pair of guards glared at us from their post.

"Violence seems to be the answer to many problems here," Spiros commented.

"And all we are left with are the questions," Xander returned.

DESERTS OF THE DRAGONS

I glanced around at the tense faces of my companions. "So there's not usually this many guards?"

Xander shook his head. "No. Much has changed since my last visit here, and I do not believe they are for the better."

We walked up the winding road. I heard a rush of wings and a pigeon flew overhead to the high temple.

"So pigeons can fly in this heat, but dragons can't?" I mused.

"They have feathers to protect their wings," Xander pointed out.

There were no guards to meet us at the top of the acropolis, but Xander pursed his lips as he perused the area. The road led into an open area that was surrounded by the majestic buildings. The largest of them loomed up before us some fifty yards off.

I slid up beside him and nudged his arm. "I know that look. Something's wrong."

He nodded. "The Jame is a celebration of the High City. For days before the festival night pilgrims climb the road to present offerings to the water goddess, Alihat Dhahabia."

I glanced around. "So where are the pilgrims?"

"They are currently barred from the High City," a voice spoke up.

We looked to our left as the familiar figure of Apuleius walked out of one of the smaller buildings. He wore his colorful green robe and walked with a spry gate, but there was a tense smile on his face as he joined us and bowed his head to Xander.

"It is good to see you are safe, My Lord. I had heard your caravan was attacked," he commented.

Xander returned the bow. "It was, but my friends and I defeated them. But what of the Jame? Why have the pilgrims been barred from the High City?"

Apuleius's smile slipped off his face. He half-turned and gestured to the most majestic of the buildings. "If you would follow me then I will explain all."

CHAPTER 11

Apuleius led us through the collection of buildings to the former residence of the ruler of Hadia. The soft white rock sparkled more brilliantly up close so I had to shield my eyes with one hand to look at the smooth sides and glistening glass windows. We walked under the archway to a pair of large wood doors. Apuleius rapped on them in a queer, rhythmic way, and they were opened by more guards. We walked past them as they watched us with suspicion deep in their eyes.

The interior of the palace was as white, but the sunlight was muffled by the soft glaze in the windows. From floor to ceiling was a distance of twenty feet, and our footsteps echoed loudly down the long halls. The way branched down three passages, the right, left and forward. Apuleius led us forward. A few other robed figures passed us with their arms stacked with books, but otherwise the halls were empty

"Am I correct to assume you have heard the rumors of the desert?" he asked us without turning around.

"We experienced for ourselves the thieves who appear from nowhere, but do you also speak of the suns among the temple buildings?" Xander asked him.

He nodded. "Yes, but those are only a few of the problems. Your yourself experienced the thieves who now roam the desert with impunity."

"I've never seen a thief use the naqia like that," Tillit spoke up.

Apuleius paused and turned to us. We stood in a rounded intersection where the path branches off in all four directions. Down the way I could see a pair of doors that reached to the tall ceiling.

"You are correct. Until a few weeks ago, the thieves attacked using hadabs as their means of transport," Apuleius told us.

"I thought the dragons in this area couldn't fly," I commented.

"That is why they use the storms created by the naqia. Their own wings aren't capable of a ground-start, but they are capable of gliding," Apuleius explained.

"Riding the storm of the naqia is a desperate way to attack someone," Spiros spoke up.

I snorted. "It almost got us."

"But they wouldn't have anywhere to go if they didn't beat who they were trying to steal from," Tillit pointed out.

Xander turned to the priest. "Then can we assume these raids have been preplanned?"

Apuleius nodded. "We in the Temple believe that is so, but we have no proof that is true other than the attacks themselves."

"Who else have they attacked?" Xander asked him.

"Wealthy Jame travelers, and there was a shipment of books that was waylaid," Apuleius admitted.

"What kind of books?"

Apuleius shook his head. "Nothing that would arouse suspicion. They were merely ancient notes on the creation of the portal. Useless information except for those with the highest skills in magic."

"Had all those who were attacked come from Wahat Alrraei?" Xander wondered.

Apuleius arched an eyebrow. "They had, but you cannot suspect Alzalam of any treachery."

Xander shook his head. "No, but the final words of one who attacked us advised us to ask Sinbad what he knew about the raid. And there is this." He drew out the sword from his waist and handed it to Apuleius. "All the thieves used one."

Apuleius studied the blade and furrowed his brow. "This is a fine weapon for a thief to wield."

My dragon lord nodded. "Yes, and that is why we suspect someone of great importance gives them aid with weapons and information."

"I will ask the local smiths if any created this blade," Apuleius offered.

Xander took the blade and returned it to his waist. "It would be better if the priests remained neutral in this search, especially if Alzalam's nephew is implicated in the matter. The residents would not look kindly on one so powerful being investigated by the temple."

Apuleius pursed his lips, but nodded. "Unfortunately, you are correct. We have never been popular in the area, and our standing has only worsened over the last month."

"People get mad when you close their temple," Tillit spoke up.

He shook his head. "The closure was in response to the threats. A month ago we began to receive these-" he reached his hand into his robe and drew out a packet of yellowed envelopes which he handed to Xander.

Xander opened one of them and read the short letter aloud. "Free the sacred home of Alihat Dhahabia of your blasphemy or die by the sword. You have thirty days to leave."

"All the high priests of the temple received the same threatening notes," Apuleius added. He stared intently at Xander. "Even the Red priest."

Xander whipped his head up to look at the priest with a frown. "They all say the same thing?"

Apuleius nodded. "They do, but with each letter the time grows shorter. The day of judgment is set for the Jame tomorrow."

"So you decided to make everyone mad by closing the temple?" Tillit commented.

Apuleius pursed his lips. "Not exactly. We first placed many guards around the temple and the city, but the letters continued to appear. They even managed to hide them in our bed chambers."

"Is the Red priest still in the city?" Xander asked him.

Apuleius nodded. "He is. He manages a copy shop now in the market, but I cannot imagine why they would involve him. He no longer has any connection to the temple other than through our books."

DESERTS OF THE DRAGONS

I leaned toward Darda who stood beside me and lowered my voice to a whisper. "Who's this Red priest guy?"

"He is the former priest who managed the affairs of the fallen dragon lord," she told me.

"Is there anyone other than the Red priest who might bear a grudge against the temple?" Xander wondered.

A bitter smile slipped onto Apuleius's lips. "I do not know if my former comrade bears a grudge, but we could pass the whole of the temple's wealth on to the citizens and they would still resent our presence. So long as we hold the temple there will always be those who despise us for our intrusion."

"Once an intruder, always an intruder," Tillit spoke up.

Darda glared at him. "Have you no respect?"

He held up his hands. "I'm just telling the truth here, Dard. Nobody likes a sore winner, and the priests haven't exactly been modest about owning the place."

She balled her hands into fists at her sides. "The priests have not harmed."

"He is correct," Apuleius interrupted her. He closed his eyes and shook his head. "While my predecessors did not physically harm anyone after the capture they have been less than kind in keeping the temple closed to them except during the Jame."

Xander tucked the note back into its envelope and handed the bundle back to Apuleius. "I would advise you to open the temple to the pilgrims, but to keep yourselves close at all times."

"But we cannot ignore the threats, My Lord," Apuleius pointed out.

Xander half-turned and glanced over our small group. "We will investigate the threats, and the attack in the desert."

Apuleius bowed his head. "As you wish, My Lord. We will send messengers across the city to inform the pilgrims that the temple is open for worship." A small smile slipped onto his lips as he looked over us. "Now if you wish I might take you to your rooms, or perhaps you would like a show of the temple complex?"

I leaned to one side and glanced past the priest at the huge entrance. I nodded at the pair of tall wood doors. "I'd like to know what's behind those doors."

Apuleius half-turned and studied at where I looked. "It is the reason this temple had a water goddess. If My Lady would allow, I will gladly show you what lies beyond."

I looked to Xander. "Any chance at a break before we go hunting for assassins and extortionists?"

He smiled and nodded. "A slight break, if only to show you your heritage."

Apuleius arched an eyebrow as he glanced between Xander and me. "Her heritage, My Lord?"

"For another time in less conspicuous surroundings, but for now show us the inner sanctum," Xander commanded him.

"Very well, My Lord."

CHAPTER 12

We walked up to the large doors with Apuleius at the forefront. He stopped before the pair and held up his hand, but not to knock. The priest bowed his head and whispered a few words. A soft green light pulsed out of his hand. The doors responded by glowing with the same color of light. I heard the clink of dozens of locks as they were unbound. Those were followed by a groan as the doors swung open to reveal a large chamber.

Apuleius dropped his hand and straightened, but he breathed hard.

Tillit rubbed his hairy chin. "So that's the legendary Lock of Priest. So only you priest guys can unlock it, right?"

Apuleius turned to him and gave a weak smile. "That is correct. It is another source of vexation for the citizens," he admitted.

I looked past Apuleius at the interior of the room. The smooth walls were the same white as the exterior of the building, but they curved up into a large dome that allowed sunlight to pierce the interior without hindrance. The bright light shot straight down and focused itself on the center of the room where stood a large pool. Two-foot tall walls surrounded the pool, but that couldn't stop the pool from reflecting its bright blue color on the walls.

In the middle of the pool stood a pedestal of marble. Atop the pedestal was a statue of a seated woman. She was naked but for the cloth tossed over one shoulder that draped most of her front to slip between her legs and pool down at her feet. Her head was bowed so that she looked into the pool beneath her, and one hand was outstretched as though to touch the water. The effect was so lifelike that for a moment I thought it was a real woman.

Apuleius stepped inside the room and gestured to the area. "This is the Sacred Temple which all pilgrims of the Jame visit. It is said that many thousands of years ago the ancestors of the city's inhabitants were in search of good water. They rested for a night on this very hilltop as a means of security and prayed to any god that they might find water soon for their skins were nearly empty. That very night they were visited by their water goddess, Alihat Dhahabia, who touched the ground and created this pool of water. She promised them that so long as their faith in her remained strong they would never want for water. They have kept their word, as has she, and from here the entire city is supplied with clean water."

I felt mesmerized as I moved past my companions and into the room. The air was cool and moist. I was drawn to the edge of the pool. The water was crystal-clear and perfectly still. My reflection stared back at me with wide eyes.

I stretched my hand out toward the pool. My fingers brushed against the surface of the water. Ripples formed beneath them, but also inside me. A tremor of refreshing coolness flowed through me. I gasped and drew my hand back.

Apuleius moved to stand beside me. He spoke in a soft voice as he studied my face. "My Lady?"

I shook myself and turned to him. My companions surrounded me, all with concerned expressions on their face but for Tillit. He was curious.

"What? What's wrong?" I asked them.

Xander set his hands on my shoulders. "You have been standing here for a few minutes staring into the water. I could not shake you from the spell."

I frowned at him. "I have not. I just touched-" I lifted my hand to show him the water, but they were dry. I blinked my digits. "I did touch it, didn't I?"

"Yes, but a long while ago," Apuleius told me.

"After which you stood there like that statue," Tillit added as he nodded at the centerpiece of the pond.

"Perhaps it is the heat," Darda suggested.

Xander glanced at Apuleius. "Would you please show us to our rooms?"

The priest nodded. "Certainly, My Lord. Please follow me."

"But I'm fine!" I insisted as I was led away. I looked over my shoulder at the peaceful waters. There came that same tugging sensation. "Nothing happened!"

"You have lost time without knowing how. That is not 'nothing,'" Xander argued as we left the sacred room.

Apuleius shut the doors behind us, but he didn't lock them before he strode down the hall. Xander gently guided me along the corridor behind the aged priest.

I crossed my arms and cast a side-glare at him. "I'm fine. Really."

"That may be so, but a short rest will improve your condition," he returned.

I rolled my eyes, but saw that arguing would be useless. Apuleius led us through the maze of corridors to the far west wing of the palace. There were more doors along the narrower corridors there, and more people. Men with short hair and attired in gray robes trudged the stone halls. They stepped to the side as we approached and bowed their heads to us.

Apuleius stopped before a group of doors and gestured to them. "These will be where you will be staying. Since this is a sacred temple we have roomed the women together away from the men to avoid sullying the holiness with fornication."

I raised my hand. "So you priest guys don't have sex?"

He smiled and bowed his head. "That is correct. We have given ourselves over to the duty of our lords. Desires of the flesh would only hinder our duties."

"When's the food served around here?" Tillit spoke up.

"Our meals are served at six in the morning, the noon hour and at seven in the evening. If you need anything please feel free to ask."

"I would like a word with you in private," Xander requested.

"I'd like to be in on that private conversation," I spoke up.

Xander smiled at me. "It is merely a matter of duty, the details of which would bore you."

I narrowed my eyes at him. "A 'duty' isn't done in secret."

He gently took me by the shoulders and set me before the door to my room. "Then I will inform you of the details at a later time, perhaps before bed when you need help to sleep."

I crossed my arms over my chest and studied him. "Then I'm expecting you to give me that bedtime story tonight."

He stepped back to stand beside Apuleius and bowed his head. "As you wish."

Darda slipped her arm around my waist. "Come. Let us rest."

She opened the door and walked me across the threshold, but I glanced over my shoulder at Xander as he and his priest strode down the hall. Darda shut the door behind us, shutting off my view of the hall. I turned my attention to the square room and found the space spartan, but clean. There were two cots with plain white blankets and pillows, and a nightstand between them. On the left side was a crude dresser with two drawers. A single small, rectangular rug close to the door finished the decor.

"Looks homey," I commented as I strode over to the right-hand bed.

"The priests prefer spiritual food to the comforts of living," Darda commented.

I plopped down on the bed and rolled onto my side. Something jabbed my hip. I winced and rummaged through my pocket. My hand touched something smooth and round. I pulled out the Soul Stone given to me by Thorontur.

I glared at it. "Then there's this stupid thing. It's been nothing but trouble since I got it."

"A Soul Stone is not a burden, but a gift," Darda scolded me.

I snorted. "Some gift. I can't even get it to work."

"Perhaps Master Apuleius can explain how to use its power," she suggested.

An idea flashed in my mind. I stood and stuffed the ball back into my pocket. "That's not a bad idea. I think I'll go find him right now."

"But Xander is-"

"Just talking about duties. I should be able to interrupt that for a few minutes," I countered as I strode toward the entrance.

Darda stepped between me and the door. "Then I will go with you."

"I'll be fine," I insisted.

She shook her head. "Your eyes tell me a different story, Miriam. They tell me the truth, and the truth is you wish to see the sanctum."

I crossed my arms and glared at her. "All right, I want to go see the pond again. What's the big deal?"

"You are part water spirit. No one can tell how such a sacred pool will effect you a second time," she pointed out.

"It didn't do anything bad to me the first time."

"You *lost* time, Miriam."

"You're not going to let me through without coming with me, are you?"

"No."

I dropped my arms and sighed. "All right, let's go."

We slipped out into the hall and Darda eased the door shut behind us. The passage was empty, so we hurried down to the first intersection. I glanced up and down the hall. There was no sign of a map.

DESERTS OF THE DRAGONS

I looked to Darda who stood by my side. "You don't happen to know where they might be, do you?"

She shook her head. "No."

I pursed my lips and lifted my foot to step out. Footsteps caught my attention and I drew back. A procession of gray-hooded men soon appeared from down the left-hand hall. Each of them held a stack of books in their arms as they marched past us.

"Somebody sure is reading a lot," I commented.

"There are a great many pilgrims in the city who would wish for a souvenir from the library," Darda pointed out.

"You think maybe one of them would know where Apuleius might be?"

"That is a possibility."

I grabbed her hand and tugged her in the direction they'd come. "Then let's go find some more."

The long passage led deep into the palace-temple. I noticed that the central passages curved around the sanctum while the outer halls led straight. The few doors were spaced far apart. My mind wasn't too adept at architecture, but there was something amiss in this design.

I glanced at Darda who walked on my left. "Don't you think-" We rounded a corner and I collided with another speed-walker.

Books clattered to the ground at our feet. There was a soft curse from my gray-clad victim as he sat up.

I stooped down and scooped up the books. "Sorry about that."

"It's quite all right. I should not have been so hasty," the man replied as he knelt in front of me.

I lifted my head and smiled at him. "Ditto."

His eyes widened as he beheld my face. I saw that the left half of his own had been scorched by a terrible fire. The skin had regrown, but was a bright pink. His left eye was cloudy.

There was a tremble in his lips as he mouthed a single, whispered word. "Marcus."

I blinked at him. "Come again?"

He shook himself and cleared his throat. I saw he was a man of fifty with short, graying hair and a short beard. "I-I'm sorry. You just reminded me of someone."

I held out his books. "I doubt it. I've never been here before."

The man took the books and studied me for a moment before he shook his head. "No, I don't believe you have. But can I help you with something?"

I looked past him at the hall. "We were kind of hoping to find Apuleius somewhere around here."

He stood and bowed his head. "I will gladly take you to him as an apology."

I grinned and stood. "It's a deal."

CHAPTER 13

The gray-clad man led us back the way he came.

"So you been here long?" I asked him.

"Thirty years," he told me.

I glanced at the books in his hands. "So are you still in training?"

"Miriam," Darda scolded me.

The man glanced over his shoulder and smiled at us. "The question is very appropriate. We in the temple are always fond of saying that there is no end to our training. Life constantly gives us new lessons to learn."

I leaned to one side and studied the cover of the top book. The title was in gold-colored lettering. "So you're reading about the portals?"

He covered the title with his hand. "It is not I who wish to read the book, but a client who wishes for it to be copied." He turned his head to one side and studied me with one eye. "But might I ask what brings you to the temple? The Jame has been canceled."

I shrugged. "We're just two women out to have some fun."

Darda frowned at me. "Miriam."

"Well, one woman out to have some fun."

My companion cleared her throat. "You must forgive my charge, Brother-"

He chuckled. "You will have to excuse me, as well, as I haven't introduced myself. I am Philo, friend to all."

Darda bowed her head to him. "It is a pleasure to meet you, Brother Philo. This-" she gestured to me, "-is Lady Miriam of Alexandria, and I am her servant, Darda."

He arched an eyebrow. "I see. That is why the good Father Apuleius has granted you a stay in the temple. Does that mean the venerable Lord Xander is also here?"

I glanced over the smooth, endless walls with their few doors. "He's here somewhere."

A crooked smile curled onto his lips. "Than it is a pleasure to escort such fine guests in his place as your guardian."

I frowned at him. "I can guard myself."

He bowed his head as we walked through the temple. "My apologies. Your physique is very deceptive."

I lifted a hand and looked at it. "It's not really my physique that-ooph." I glared at Darda who'd jabbed me in the ribs. "What's that-" She gave me a warning glance. I sighed and dropped my hand. "Anyway, where's Apuleius's room?"

Philo nodded at a coming door some ten yards off. There was a slight green tinge in the wood. "That is his room."

I grabbed his shoulder and smiled at him. "Thanks. We'll take it from here."

He arched an eyebrow, but bowed his head. "Very well."

Our guide left us, but Darda, too, stared at me with a quizzical expression. "Are you sure you are not in need of a rest, Miriam?"

I pressed my finger to my lips and pointed at the door. She frowned, but I didn't pay it any heed as I crept toward the entrance. I pressed one ear against the thick, woody surface and listened.

The door swung open and I toppled forward onto the hard stone floor of the room. I rolled over and glared up at Xander who stood behind the door with his hand still on the handle. There was a sly smile on his lips.

"Would you like to come in?" Xander teased.

I climbed to my feet and brushed myself off. "You could have warned me."

Darda stepped inside and Xander closed the door. "I thought perhaps you had forgotten how to knock," he returned.

I looked at our surroundings. There was a simple cot-like bed with a short dresser and a small table. Apuleius was seated in one of the two chairs around a small table. On the table were two small glasses of drink.

Xander strode past me and took his drink in hand before he turned to me. "You decided you were not in need of a rest?"

"I am sorry, Xan-" Darda's eyes flickered to the amused face of Apuleius, "-My Lord, but My Lady-" Xander held up his empty hand and shook his head.

"I understand, Darda. Your mistress is very headstrong," he agreed.

I crossed my arms and glared at me. "And curious. I wanted to know what you two were talking about."

Xander glanced over his shoulder at Apuleius. "If you would continue with what you were saying, Apuleius."

The priest bowed his head. "Yes, My Lord. As I was saying, the bonded natural magic was then combined with the blood of all the dragon lords, thus bringing about a reaction beyond of nature and yet against-"

"Wait a second," I spoke up as I held up a hand. I looked to Xander but pointed at Apuleius. "What's he talking about?"

"Apuleius was giving me a brief lesson on the magic used to create the Portal," he explained.

"And it's that dry?"

Apuleius smiled. "Not all magic is beautiful, and some of it can be very dull."

"Did you wish to join in on the conversation?" Xander wondered.

I cringed and backed up only to bump into Darda. "I think we'll be going."

"Miriam, did you not have a question for his holiness?" Darda whispered to me.

My eyes widened. "Oh! Right!" I dug around in my pocket and pulled out the Soul Stone. I held it out to Apuleius. "How do I use this?"

His eyes widened as he beheld the round stone and he stood. "Is that a Soul Stone?"

I nodded. "Yeah. King Thorontur gave it to me."

He walked up to me and held out his hand. "May I see it?" I dropped the stone into his hand. Apuleius pinched the stone between his thumb and index finger, and examined the fine green color. "Magnificent."

"But not useful," I added.

He smiled at me. "I have heard that Soul Stones are rather difficult to use. Some on whom the gift is bestowed never unlock its secret power."

My face fell. "So it might just be a stone my entire life?"

He nodded as he handed the stone back. "Yes, but do not look upon that as a bad consequence. Soul Stones are granted for great and dangerous deeds done on behalf of fae. It is only through more great and dangerous deeds that its true power can be revealed."

I winced and stuffed the stone back into my pocket. "You're right. I think I'll be happy with a quiet life." I glanced over my shoulder at Xander and Darda. "Unfortunately, I don't think I'm going to get any of that here."

Apuleius looked past me and at my companions. "Might I be so bold as to ask why you have a sudden interest in the Portal, My Lord?"

Xander pursed his lips as his eyes fell on me. "It is because of my Maiden that I ask."

Apuleius arched an eyebrow. "Has there been some complication with her traveling into our world?"

"Just a little wet and wild trouble," I quipped.

The priest furrowed his brow. "I do not understand."

"My Maiden has been found to be part Mare Fae," Xander admitted.

Apuleius's eyes widened as they fell on me. "Indeed? That is quite a rare honor, but I do not understand how she is one without being of our world."

"But I might be," I told him. I looked at the floor and furrowed my brow as I thought of the memories Valtameri had allowed me to see. "At least, I think that's what I saw. Valtameri couldn't really release all of my memories."

The priest started back. "Valtameri? The lord of the oceans?"

"Perhaps we had better start at the beginning, but I must ask for the utmost secrecy in this matter," Xander commanded.

Apuleius resumed his seat and nodded. "You have it, now and forever, My Lord."

"Then let me begin."

CHAPTER 14

Xander recapped for our priestly friend the trials and revelations of our last watery adventure. By the time the tale was done Apuleius's lips were tightly pursed.

"If it is true that My Lady's father created a portal than that would indeed be a grave crime against our world," he commented.

"And Miriam would not be spared a portion of the punishment," Xander finished for him.

Apuleius closed his eyes and shook his head. "No. The rules are not well written, as such a breach is considered a reckless use of magic even by those who study the Portal's magic, but she would be interrogated in order to learn of her father and what he may have done to our world."

I felt the color drain from my face. "What kind of interrogation?"

Apuleius looked me in the eyes. "They would probe your memories for such clues, even to the verge of your losing your mind. The process is undoubtedly painful, and even if your mind is not broken then your body may suffer ill-effects."

I whipped my head to Xander. "I think I want to leave now."

He pursed his lips as his attention lay on his priest. "Do you have the skill to release the barrier in her mind of which Valtameri spoke?"

"It would be impossible to know without probing her mind," Apuleius replied.

"But you said that it would hurt me," I reminded him.

He stood and smiled at me. "I will be as gentle as I can, My Lady."

I looked to Xander. He nodded. My shoulders slumped and I sighed. "All right, but I better not come out not being able to count to three."

Apuleius stepped up to me and placed his palm on my forehead. "Please relax, My Lady."

My derisive snort was interrupted by a strange push against my forehead. It wasn't the gentle intrusion of Valtameri. This felt like a hand wiggled into my brain and started poking and prodding every squishy part of it. I shut my eyes and ground my teeth as he probed the inner depths of my memories. Faint images skimmed across my closed eyelids like a bad family-trip slide show.

A sensation made me gasp. It felt like he hit a bump in my brain. He prodded a little harder. I winced a little more as a sharp pain began to build at the front of my mind. The more he pushed the more it thumped. The pressure built higher and higher. I felt like my brain was going to burst. A flash of light washed over my eyes.

The pain was gone. I opened my eyes. The spartan room was gone. In its place was the sanctum with its calm pool. Before the pool stood a gray-hooded figure. Their head was bent down so I could only see the lower half of their face, but that was enough to recognize the strong jaw of a man. He had a smile much like my own.

"My little Estelwen. You've grown so much."

I frowned and took a step toward him. "Do I know you?"

He chuckled. There was no mirth in the sound. "You do, and yet you don't. I'm with you every day, but I've been dead for nearly you're entire life."

I blinked at him. "Come again?"

He raised his head a little. I could make out the tip of his nose and his strong cheekbones, but his eyes remained hidden. His lips were pursed. "I wish I had more time to talk to you, but there is little left. You can't break the seal on your memories. Not yet. I planted the spell as a protection for you, and only when you're ready to protect yourself can you break it. Do you understand?"

I shook my head and took another step toward him. "No, I don't understand. Who are you? What do you mean you're always with me? Why'd you lock my memories away?"

The scene around me grew dim as though a heavy curtain fell over the walls on either side of me. The darkness closed in on the hooded figure. He raised his head a little more and showed himself to be a young man of perhaps twenty-five with short dark hair. A bitter smile showed on his lips as his brown eyes shone at me. "Until we meet again, my little Estelwen, beware the friend."

I rushed forward and stretched out my arm toward him. Something pulled me back even as the darkness swallowed him. "Wait! Don't go!"

The pain was back. Apuleius's hand was once again on my forehead. The warning from the man echoed in my aching head.

I reached out and grabbed Apuleius's wrist. My voice was hoarse as I pleaded with him. "No more."

He hovered his hand a little above my forehead. "Are you sure?"

I nodded. "Yeah."

Apuleius lowered his hand and I inched open one of my eyes. His lips were pursed. Xander came up beside me and grasped my shoulders. He leaned down and studied my face. "Are you all right?"

I rubbed my temple and winced as the last throbbing bit of pain disappeared. The tears in my eyes, however, were a little more difficult to wipe away. "I-I think so."

Xander looked to Apuleius. "Did you manage to break the seal?"

The priest shook his head. "No. There is a very powerful protective magic on her earliest memories."

"What is it protected by?" Xander asked him.

Apuleius studied me. "The protection is not for the spell, but for her."

I started back. Xander noticed, but Darda spoke up. "What do you mean, Your Holiness?"

"The spell within My Lady is not permanent. From what I gathered, it is meant to be released at some point in her life."

I swallowed the lump in my throat and raised my head. "He said it would go away when I was ready."

My friends stared at me quizzically. Xander pulled me against him. "Who told you that?"

"My dad. He just came to me and told me not to undo the spell until I was ready to protect myself."

Apuleius's eyes never left me as he slowly nodded his head. "I see. That explains the strength of the spell. Only a deep bond can create such a powerful force that even my magic could not break."

"Could it be that one of your former priests was Miriam's father?" Xander asked him.

Apuleius stroked his beard. "That is quite likely. No one but my brothers are fluent in the portal magic. However, I would need to refer to the registry of brothers in the library to be sure of the man's identity. We might go now, if you wish."

"Perhaps My Lady would like a rest?" Darda suggested.

I stood straighten and shook my head. "I'm fine. Besides, I couldn't take a nap knowing I was going to find my father."

Apuleius gestured to the door. "Then if you will all follow me."

CHAPTER 15

We stepped out into the hall and met two of our forgotten company, Tillit and Spiros. They stopped before us and Spiros bowed his head. "My apologies, My Lord, but I was concerned when you did not return."

Tillit grinned and gave us a lazy salute. "I thought you might have gotten into trouble, too, so I followed him."

Apuleius smiled at our two friends. "Quite the contrary. We were on our way to the library."

Tillit stepped back and waved. "If that's all then I'll be taking my leave. Books never were a very profitable endeavor for me."

Darda crossed her arms and glared at him. "They would have done a great deal to improve that mind of yours."

"But not my pocketbook, so I'll be seeing you." He turned and strode down the hall.

DESERTS OF THE DRAGONS

Xander looked to his captain with a sly smile on his lips. "If the books also frighten you, I give you leave to return to your room."

Spiros grinned and shrugged. "I must go many places where you have never trod to follow you, My Lord."

Apuleius shook his head and chuckled. "If you will follow me."

He led us through the maze that was the white palace. The library lay in the direction of the northwest corner of the building. We reached an intersection that led out of the sleeping quarters and either left toward the front way or right deeper into the labyrinth. A hard, loud clap of footsteps on the marble floors made us look to our left.

A gray-hooded young man hurried down the hall toward our group. He stopped before us, winded and breathing hard, and bowed his head to Apuleius. "Your Holiness, the gates have been opened and the city alerted as you commanded, but the number of pilgrims far exceeds what the temple can hold."

Apuleius pursed his lips. "Have you shut one of the doors?"

The man nodded. "We have, Your Holiness, but many of the locals forced it open again. They also refuse to obey our commands to line up single file so they may see the sanctum."

Apuleius turned to us. "I fear I cannot escort you as I promised."

Xander shook his head. "You are needed elsewhere by many more people. I know the way to the library, but what reference must we find."

"The librarian keeps the registry under key. Merely ask him for the registry, and he will gladly allow you to view its pages," Apuleius told us.

"Your Holiness," the young man persisted.

Apuleius bowed his head to us. "If you will excuse me." He hurried down the hall with the young man close at his heels.

Xander glanced at Spiros. "They may need your help."

Spiros frowned. "I would rather remain here."

My dragon lord set his hand on Spiros's shoulder and smiled. "We are in the temple of the dragon lords. Aside from Alexandria, there is no safer place in the world for us to be."

"Alexandria is safe because she is well-protected," Spiros countered.

Xander slipped his hand down to Spiros's back and gave his old friend a push down the hall. "That is an order, captain."

Spiros glanced over his shoulder. "Then swear you will not leave the temple."

Our dragon lord bowed his head. "I swear it, now hurry."

Spiros turned away and hurried down the hall where Apuleius had gone. I looked at Xander. "He's really worried about something, isn't he?"

Xander pursed his lips and gave a nod. "Yes. It may have something to do with the thieves in the desert."

I arched an eyebrow. "What about them?"

Xander led our group of three down the right-hand hall that led deeper into the temple. "As you know, the thieves used expensive weapons, the kind only a wealthy patron could give to loyal men."

DESERTS OF THE DRAGONS

Darda snorted. "Men indeed. More like cutthroats."

Xander glanced at her and smiled. "Someone thought them worry of the trouble and expense to give them all new weapons." He looked around us at the well-washed walls and occasional statue. "The temple itself is the wealthiest entity in the area."

Darda's eyes widened and her mouth dropped open. "Surely you do not believe the temple to be involved, My Lord! The priests and brothers here would do no such monstrosity!"

He shook his head. "I cannot be so confident in your assessment. Many were once members or friends to the Red Dragon, and they might have been corrupted by his influence and lying in wait for a time to make their true intentions known."

"But what of the thief's last words? He asked us to inquire of Sinbad what he knew," she reminded him.

I raised my hand. "If some of these guys worked for the Red Dragon then shouldn't they have gotten rid of them?"

Xander pursed his lips. "There were too many apprenticed brothers to the Red Dragon to disregard their teaching. Rather than order them to leave, they were given over to other dragon-" He froze.

Darda and I walked a few steps and turned to face Xander. His eyes were wide and his teeth were clenched so tightly his lips were white.

I frowned and took a step toward him. "What's-" Xander spun around.

I saw a flicker of gray behind him before a brilliant flash of red light crashed into Xander's chest. A sudden pain stabbed at my shoulder and made me cry out.

Xander fell backward. I ignored the pain and caught him before he dropped to the ground. My eyes widened as I beheld a large smoldering circle in the center of his chest. His clothes were burnt away so that I could see his charred flesh. The putrid stench filled my nostrils. His breathing was short and harsh, but it was there. His eyes were scrunched shut and he grit his teeth.

I shook his shoulders. "Xander! Xander, wake up!"

Darda stepped up to me and removed a pair of daggers from her dress. "Run, Miriam."

I looked up with tears streaming down my face. "Run? What are you-" I saw she looked behind us, and followed her gaze.

Before her stood a half dozen gray-cloaked figures. Their faces were covered in the shadows of their gray hoods. One of them lowered their hand from which came a few puffs of smoke. They took a step toward us.

"Run, Miriam!" Darda commanded me.

I frowned and shook my head. "I'm not leaving you! Either of you!"

Darda threw one of her daggers. A different cloaked figure threw up one arm. From his open hand erupted a fireball. The ball hit the dagger and incinerated it. The ashes fell worthless to the floor at their feet.

Darda grabbed my shoulder with one hand while her other gripped her dagger. She pulled me to my feet and shoved me down the hall. I stumbled forward but caught myself and half-turned to her. She stepped between the coming brothers and me. "Run! I will distract them!"

"But-"

DESERTS OF THE DRAGONS

Darda glanced over her shoulder and smiled. "If they had wished me dead then I would not have been spared with the dagger. I will bide you time, but run! Run now!"

I swallowed the lump in my throat and took a step away from her without looking away. "Fine, but don't you dare die on me."

She bowed her head and returned her attention to the cloaked figures. I turned away and raced down the hall, but before I took a turn I glanced over my shoulder.

Darda was throwing her whole arsenal of daggers at them. Many were incinerated before impact, but others forced the figures to duck into side corridors. Most reappeared and threw their fireballs at Darda and her daggers. A few didn't peek back around the corner.

A loose fireball threw past my head. I took that as a signal to leave, and raced around the corner. A long, empty corridor awaited me. My feet pounded against the hard stone as I flew past the few wooden doors. Another intersection loomed up ahead.

So did a gray-cloaked figure. One of the brothers stepped out from the corridor on my left and right into my path. For a moment my heart skipped a beat in hope, but that was soon dashed when I noticed their face was covered with their hood. I skidded to a stop and took a step back as he walked toward me.

I whipped my head left and right. Lady Luck was on my side. There was a door just to my left, one I hadn't noticed before. I swung it open and dove in without looking. My feet stumbled on the uneven stones and I crashed to the floor.

A pair of feet walked up and stopped in front of me. I lifted my head. My eyes widened.

Standing above me was the kindly librarian, Crates. There was a smile on his face as he leaned down and offered me his hand. "You have had quite a chase, haven't you?"

I looked around myself. The familiar countless rows of books lined the walls with their circular balconies before them. In the center of the room was the floating bridge with its circular endpoint.

I took his hand and he pulled me to my feet. "How. . .?" I whispered as I looked into his gentle face.

"A door is ever there for one who needs it," he quoted. He looked past me and the smile slipped from his lips. "

I turned and my breath caught in my throat. The gray-cloaked man from the hallway stood in the open doorway gaping at the view.

"You must leave, sir. It was not you who was meant to use the door," the librarian told him.

My pursuer shook himself free of his stupor and stepped inside. "Not without the woman."

Crates raised one hand and beckoned with one finger towards himself. The door closed with a loud clang that made the man, and me, jump. The man swung around and fumbled for the knob. No amount of tugging would pull it open.

The man spun around and glared at Crates. "Release the seal!"

Crates shook his head as he drew me back toward the railing. "I am afraid I cannot do as you demand. You must be punished for your transgression."

A loud screeching noise echoed through the library. The man and I looked up into the tall tiers. A shadow swooped down from the ceiling. The torches that lit the area reflected on a pair of pale wings and talons.

DESERTS OF THE DRAGONS

Crates leaned toward me and lowered his voice. "I would suggest you look away. This won't be pleasant."

I couldn't. Another screech sounded through the hall as the shadow flew over our heads. A wind beneath its wings blew my hair over my eyes. I swept the strands out of my face and my eyes widened.

Between the man and us stood a griffin. Its elegant white wings were folded against its furry back. The long claws on its paws tapped against the stone floor as it snapped its eagle jaws at the man. The shimmering light of its bright yellow eyes watched the man like the eagle it was.

My cloaked pursuer stumbled back and drew out both hands. Fires lit up in his palms as the griffin took a step toward him.

"S-stay back! Back!" he screamed.

The griffin kept stalking toward him. He threw one of his fireballs. The flames splashed over the creature's face. The griffin paused and screeched in anger before it lunged at him. He threw a barrage of fireballs at the griffin as the creature barreled down at him.

He disappeared in a flurry of claws and feathered. I looked away as the man screamed. His cries were cut short. I peeked at the door. The griffin turned around and pawed at its bloody beak. There was no other trace that the man had ever existed.

I jumped when Crates set his hand on my shoulder. "Please come with me."

I turned to him with a gaping mouth. "B-but-" He smiled and shook his head.

"The griffin will not harm you so long as you are the one who was meant to open the door. Now come and tell me what has brought you here."

CHAPTER 16

The griffin spread its wings and flapped into the air. I watched with wide eyes as the mythical creature flew over our heads and up toward the roof. The creature landed with a soft clack of its claws on top of the bookcases on the uppermost floor. It drew its wings against its body and nestled in for a long stay.

Crates moved toward the bridge, but I didn't follow. My attention was still riveted to the spot where the man had once stood before the door. He paused and looked back to me. "Are you feeling well?"

I snapped my jaws shut and spun around to face him where I pointed a finger at the empty spot. "A griffin just killed a guy, and you're asking me if I'm feeling well?"

He nodded. "I am."

I threw up my arms. "How is this not insane? How could you just let that thing kill him like that? What the hell is a griffin doing in a library?"

Crates turned fully to me and studied my face. "The Library is filled with books that contain great power, and with that comes a great responsibility to protect that power. The griffin and I protect the Library so that none but the worthy may partake of the knowledge contained within these walls." He looked past me at the empty spot. "I could sense he had nothing but malice toward you, one who is worthy of visiting the Library, and Justum, the creature you witnessed, also sensed the danger and dealt with it accordingly."

I leaned back and arched an eyebrow. "You could 'sense' that?"

He smiled. "There was also your abrupt entrance and the fear in your face. I am curious to know why such an individual was pursuing you."

I looked at the ground and furrowed my brow. "I'm not really sure. We were just walking down the hall when we were attacked by those robed guys. Xander-" My eyes widened. I whipped my head around to look at the door. There was still a dull pain in my shoulder. "I have to get back! Xander was hurt!"

"He is hurt but still alive, as your shoulder attests," Crates told me as he tilted his head to one side. "But do you not wonder why you were brought here?"

I turned to him and frowned. "I don't really like riddles."

He chuckled and strode away from me toward the balcony where stood the bookshelves. His hand beckoned to me over his shoulder. "Come with me."

I pressed my palm against my shoulder, but reluctantly followed him. He led me to one of the filled shelves and pulled out a tome. Gold lettering graced the browned cover, but I couldn't read the foreign letters. "This may be of use to you."

I took it and opened the book to a random page. There was the same gibberish language. I looked up at him. "What am I supposed to do with this? I can't even read it."

Crates grabbed my shoulders and spun me around so I faced the door. "I am sure you will find someone who is able, but now you must return."

My heels slid across the floor as he pushed me to the exit. "So I have to carry this heavy thing around with me until I find someone who can?"

He paused and smiled. "You are correct. That is quite a burden, and very noticeable." He lay his palm on the cover. My eyes widened as the tome shrank to the size of a pocket dictionary. "That will be a more suitable size. Now come." He continued with his pushing.

I glared over my shoulder at him. "With those guys following me?"

"Like rats, they have returned to their hiding places. Now your friends seek you, and-" we reached the door and he opened it to reveal one of the many halls in the temple, "-it would not do to keep them waiting."

He gave me a good shove that sent me stumbling into the hall. There was a clang as the door shut behind me. I spun around and found myself facing an empty wall. The door, and that crazy guy, had vanished. All I had left of my little adventure was the book clutched against my chest.

"Miriam!"

I looked to my left. Darda was hurrying down the hall in my direction. Her clothes were scorched at the edges and her face was blackened with smoke. She was out of breath when she stumbled up to me and wrapped me in a tight hug.

"Thank goodness you are safe!" she spoke into my shoulder. She pulled us apart to arm's length and looked me over. "How did you manage to escape them?"

I smiled and held up the book. "It was all thanks to a right turn into a library."

She furrowed her brow, but shook off her confusion and set her hand on my back. "Come. The others are searching for you, and Xander is nearly frantic with worry."

"So he's okay?" I asked her as I was once again pushed rather than led.

"Yes, but he insists on-" We rounded a corner and met with a terrifying sight.

Before us and halfway down the hall was Xander. He leaned his shoulder against the left-hand wall and his skin was nearly the same white color. His breathing was harsh and he gritted his teeth, but he pulled himself along the wall with one hand while his other clutched his chest. A few flimsy bandages were wrapped around his scorched wound. The ends of the cloth hung limp as though unfinished.

"Good god!" I yelped as I rushed toward him.

He whipped his head up and his eyes widened. "Miriam!" he croaked out.

I wrapped my arms around his chest, partially to hug him and partially to hold him up. I looked into his pale face and felt the color drain from my own. "What the hell are you doing? You need to get to bed."

He weakly smiled at me. "I would not rest until I found you."

"Well, I found you, and that's good enough for both of us," I quipped as I slipped one of his arms over my shoulders. "Now let's get you to bed." I looked around us at the expanse of identical halls. "Just as soon as I remember where that is."

Darda slipped Xander's other arm over her shoulders and smiled. "I will lead the way."

We shuffled down the hall back to the residents corridor. The cot in Xander's room was narrow, but adequate. I covered him with the thin blanket up to the wound on his chest. The bandages were bloodied and I could still smell the scent of scorched flesh.

"Spiros," he whispered.

"I'm sure he's fine," I told him.

He shook his head. "No. Bring him."

"At once," Darda agreed as she drew a roll of bandages from her clothes and handed it to me. "Please finish the bandaging for me."

I didn't have time to refuse before she whisked herself away. I unrolled some of the bandages and looked down at my patient. "I don't have much experience with this."

He smiled. "I will risk the pain."

I sighed and shrugged before I leaned down. "All right, but don't say I didn't warn you."

His yelps and grunts of pain still echoed around the room when Darda and Spiros entered. Spiros hesitated only a moment on seeing his lord's wound before his eyes narrowed. He lay his hand on the hilt of his sword. "Who did this, My Lord?"

Xander shook his head. "I cannot be sure."

I snorted. "I know who it was. It was a bunch of monks."

DESERTS OF THE DRAGONS

"That cannot be proven, Miriam," Darda scolded me.

I glared at her. "They were dressed in those robes, Darda, and don't the guys around here know magic?"

Spiros looked back to Xander. "What do you intend to do?"

Xander sat up and winced. "I am not sure yet." There came a knock on the door. Xander tensed as Spiros slipped against the wall where the door would open. "Who is there?" Xander called out.

"It is me, My Lord, and my personal assistant, Philo," Apuleius replied.

Everyone relaxed, though Spiros remained by the door. "Enter," Xander answered.

Apuleius stepped into the room. Behind him followed Philo. "I saw Captain Spiros hurry away with Darda. Is there something-" His eyes fell on Xander and widened. "My Lord! What happened?"

"Just some of your monks trying to kill all of us."

Apuleius hurried to Xander's side. "Is this true?"

Xander nodded. "It is true, they were dressed in the habits of the brothers, and they stole Miriam away so quickly we must assume they were well-familiar with the temple." He touched the bandages on his chest and looked Apuleius in the eyes. "They used a very powerful fire magic that was capable of burning even my flesh."

Apuleius narrowed his eyes and pursed his lips. "I see." He turned to Philo. "Who was not present during the opening of the doors?"

Philo shook his head. "No one, Your Holiness. Everyone was called and came to assist."

"I am not mistaken," Xander insisted.

"Neither am I," I added. "And what about the guys delivering the books? Were they all there?"

Philo chuckled. "They are merely pages. Certainly they are not capable of performing the magic of which you speak."

The priest furrowed his brow and pulled at his beard. "We must find where everyone was at the time of the attack. And will you please have someone bring me the medicine from my room?"

Philo bowed his head. "As you wish, Your Holiness." He hurried from the room. Spiros made sure the door was shut firmly behind him.

Apuleius turned back to Xander and bowed his head. "I am sorry this occurred, My Lord. If you see it fit to punish me, then I-" Xander held up one hand and shook his head.

"This was not your fault, Apuleius. I believe there are other forces at work beyond our vision that pulls these strings."

Apuleius raised an eyebrow. "The Red Dragon people, My Lord?"

Xander threw off his covers and swung his legs over the side of the bed. "It is not impossible. For that reason we must investigate as much as possible as quickly as possible. We will make inquiries about the weapons while you search for the intruders. There is also the matter of the registry."

I stomped forward and put my hands on his shoulders. "*You're* not doing anything. You and Spiros can stay right here and have a long chat."

He shook his head. "It is too dangerous to separate."

"I think it's more dangerous in here than out on the streets, so Darda and I should be enough," I pointed out. "Especially if we can find out where that pig man went."

Xander looked me in the eyes. "I will not leave you alone in such dangerous circumstances."

I opened my mouth to protest, but Apuleius set his hand on my shoulder. I looked up into his smiling face. "You needn't worry for our lord. I will fetch some medicine to apply to his wounds that will heal them very quickly." He turned to leave.

"Wait a sec. There's something I need to ask you." Apuleius paused in the doorway and half-turned to me. I drew out the miniature tome and held it out to him. "I got this from Crates, that library guy. He said I needed to find somebody to read it to me."

Apuleius's eyes widened, but he took the book. "The Mallus Library?"

I shrugged. "I guess."

"It is, Your Holiness," Darda assured him.

He looked down at the book and brushed his hand over the cover. His voice was soft and quiet. "I never thought I would live long enough to touch a book from that most ancient place."

"But can you read it?" I asked him.

He studied the lettering for a moment before he shook his head. "No. Unfortunately, I cannot. It is completely unfamiliar to me."

My face fell as he handed the book back to me. "This might take a while..."

"Did he say for what purpose Crates gave you the book?" Apuleius wondered.

I tucked the book into one of my pockets and shook my head. "Nope. He just said I'd need it."

Apuleius smiled. "Then I am sure you will." There came a soft rap on the door. "Enter."

One of the young pages slipped into the room. In his hands was a small white alabaster box. He held it out to Apuleius. "The medicine, Your Holiness."

Apuleius took the box and bowed his head. "Thank you. You may leave." The man backed out of the room and shut the door behind him. Apuleius turned to Xander and opened the lid. A waft of a sweet, honey-like scent flowed over the room. "This salve will assist your wounds in healing against the magic."

I folded my arms and looked down at my dragon lord. "So there's some stuff even Xander has trouble getting through, huh?"

Apuleius set the box on the nightstand beside the bed and nodded as he took out a few fingers of the tan-colored gunk. "There is, but fortunately I have made a study of medicinal herbs. This will be done in a-" he grasped an outer bandage and my expert work fell loose onto the sheets. Apuleius blinked at the mess in his hand. "Or perhaps even faster."

I hung my head. "That was my job."

He chuckled as he unwound the few remaining bandages. "I am sure My Lord will give you much practice."

"Unfortunately. . ."

CHAPTER 17

"Wow."

The comment came from me. Xander was now smothered in goo and, with a fresh change of expertly applied bandages, we, with Darda and Spiros, hurried our way to the front entrance. A steady stream of people flowed through the right-hand door and wound their way down the hall in the direction of the sanctum. They exited out the left-hand door.

While my companions joined the throngs that left the building, I paused and glanced back at the line that went inside. A soft tug inside me told me I envied them.

Darda looped her arms around mine and tugged me along. "Do not dawdle," she scolded me.

"I wasn't dawdling, I was only looking."

"You should not enter there again."

A figure stepped out of the crowd and slunk their arm through my free one so that I was pinned between Darda and their body. "I don't think she knows what she's talking about."

I whipped my head to my left and found myself staring into the bemused face of Tillit. Darda leaned forward and glared at him. "Did anyone ask for your opinion?"

He thought for a moment before he shook his head. "Nope, but I still think you're overreacting. Fae don't hurt each other, especially when they're related."

"Perhaps the relation is too distant for them to care," she argued.

I winced. "Could you guys stop pulling before you don't have to share me?"

Darda released me. "I am sorry, Miriam, but this pig-" she glared at Tillit, "-is a bad influence."

He grinned and bowed his head. "Flattery will get you places, dear Darda."

I placed my palms on both their chests and pushed them apart. "All right, that's enough, you two. Let's catch up with everyone else."

Darda was sullen, and Tillit gleeful, as we slipped through the door and out into the bright fresh air of the early afternoon. A dry breeze swept over us and brought with it the sound of music and laughter. Our friends waited for us just outside the entrance.

Xander turned to Tillit. "We are now in need of your shop expertise."

Tillit grinned and bowed his head. "I thought you might, so I came by to see if you were done with the stiffs in there." He glanced at the hint of bandages that stuck out from beneath Xander's shirt. "Did something happen?"

"Some of those stiffs tried to give us an exciting time," I told him.

"We will tell you on the way down the hill," Xander offered.

Xander brought Tillit up to speed on our adventures as our group meandered our way down the busy highway that was the hill road. By the time we reached the bottom Xander was done and Tillit gave a whistle. "Sounds like someone wants you both out of the picture pretty bad. With service like that I'm glad I got myself a room in the town. If you ever run into that trouble again, feel free to drop by anytime. It's not much, but it is danger-free."

"In addition to the metal smiths and weapons dealers, could you lead us to the Red Dragon's priest?" Xander requested.

Tillit nodded. "Sure. He's not exactly hiding, but these streets are pretty hard to navigate."

We reached the mess of streets and went about the tedious task of inquiring at every metal smith and weapons dealer in town. For a peaceful town, there were a lot. Most were tucked into corner buildings in a small district far from the gate. Two of the walls open to the streets. The fumes of smoke and cooked metal tickled our nostrils as Xander and Tillit slipped into the first of the shops.

The rest of us stood just outside the hot zone and watched. I could still hear the faint jingle of music and laughter down some hidden street.

"Excuse me, but we wish to inquire of the wares you make," Xander explained.

The shopkeeper, a burly man with a low brow, crossed his arms and glared at us. At his side was a young apprentice. "If you're not here to buy something, then get out."

"Would you be able to make this sort of blade?" Xander asked him as he removed the thief's weapon from his waist.

The shopkeeper narrowed his eyes. "And if I can?"

Tillit slipped around the hot irons and forge. His quick eyes gathered in all the hanging finished products. "I don't think this guy's our man."

The blacksmith whipped his head around and glared at the sus. "What are you saying?"

Tillit turned to him with a grin. "I'm saying you don't make what we're looking for."

The keeper balled his hands into fists at his sides and gritted his teeth. "Are you saying I'm not good enough to make it?"

The sus's eyes flashed and his grin slipped into a sly smile. "You know who makes them, don't you?"

He turned his face away and crossed his arms over his wide chest. "I'm not saying anything."

"Has a man by the name of Sinbad made inquiries?" Xander asked him.

The blacksmith dropped one hand onto a large, thick hammer that sat on his anvil. "Enough questions. Leave."

Tillit slid up to Xander's side and leaned toward him. "In case you missed it, that's our cue to leave." He looped his arm through Xander's and led him out of the smithy and back to our small group. "Perhaps Lady Fortune will smile on us at the next shop."

I slipped up beside Xander. His lips were pursed so hard the red stood out against his pale face. "You okay?" I whispered.

He nodded. "I am fine. It is merely this wound." He pressed his palm against his chest.

DESERTS OF THE DRAGONS

"Hopefully this won't take too long," I commented as I glanced over my shoulder. The shopkeeper whispered a few words into the ear of his shop boy, who raced off down a side street. I looked back to Xander. "That guy's-um, guy just took off."

"I expected as much," Xander replied.

I arched an eyebrow. "Expected what?"

"That he would warn Sinbad about our inquiries."

I frowned. "Then why'd you bring up his name?"

Tillit looked over his shoulder and winked at me. "Because our lord here wants to make sure Sinbad comes to us, and not the other way around."

Darda pursed her lips. "That was a very reckless action to take, Xander. Secrecy would have been the more prudent approach."

Tillit laughed and clapped her on the back. "Don't be so doubtful about our ability to protect ourselves."

She steadied herself and turned up her nose at him. "You have shown very little in the ways of protecting anyone other than yourself."

He leaned toward her and winked. "Just give me the right opportunity and I'll show you what Tillit's made of."

Xander stopped and gazed straight ahead. "That time may have come."

We looked in the same direction and stiffened. The narrow street was surrounded on both sides by the walls of windowless, sun-dried clay homes. Between those walls stood a crowd of rough-looking men. At their head stood Sinbad.

His arms were crossed, as was his expression. "I was told you were asking questions about me," he told us.

Xander bowed his head. "I am glad to see that words still travel fast among the narrow streets of the city."

Sinbad dropped his arms to his side, and one of his hands landed on the hilt of a dagger that was tucked into his waistband. "You play a dangerous game, dragon lord."

Spiros lay his hand on the hilt of his own weapon. Xander stretched out his arm in front of his captain, but his eyes never left Sinbad. "What do you have to do with the thieves of the desert?"

One of the burly men, the horn blower, stepped forward and unsheathed his weapon. A grumble of disapproval arose from the other men. Sinbad held up his hand, and they were silenced.

A crooked grin slipped onto Sinbad's lips. "Who says I have anything to do with them?"

"A desert snake told us," Xander replied.

Sinbad chuckled. "Then the snake has a lot to answer for. As for you-"

The music that had kept to the background now came to the forefront as a parade rounded the corner behind us. The procession of brightly-colored festival-goers with their rattling tambourines and tooting horns flowed into our group. We pressed our backs against the sun-baked walls and watched the laughing, jostling people dance by. Many held up the small female figurines. Others clapped in time with the lively noise. A minority of the paraders walked in solemn columns with their hands clasped together and their eyes turned downward.

The noise and crowds filled the narrow alley with a disorienting mixture of gaiety and somberness. In the chaos Xander wrapped his arm around my waist and pulled me close to him. It was because of that gesture that I was able to see Sinbad slip through the crowd and pause at Xander's side and in front of him.

He leaned toward Xander. "I will tell you everything I know, but only if you join the race tomorrow."

Xander frowned. "And if I refuse?"

Sinbad shrugged. "Then you know nothing. It is your choice, but I believe we both know what you will choose. See you tomorrow."

He stepped into the parade and disappeared in the thick mess of people. I was left with a sinking feeling in my chest.

CHAPTER 18

I glanced up at Xander's pale face. His lips were pressed tightly together as he stared straight ahead at the dwindling crowd.

"What now?" I asked him.

He shook his head. "I am not sure."

Spiros with Darda and Tillit pushed their way through the tail-end of the parade and rejoined us.

"So what did the prince of the desert scorpions have to say to you?" Tillit asked us.

Xander looked in the direction the parade had gone, and along with it Sinbad and his men. "He informed me that I would know the truth if I competed in the race tomorrow."

Spiros frowned. "That sounds like a trap."

Xander slowly nodded. "It could very well be."

Tillit clapped his hands together. "Well, what say we avoid that whole killing trap and get looking at the other shops?"

"What's this race?" I spoke up.

"It's a race that reenacts the escape of the town hero with the library books," Tillit told me.

I arched an eyebrow. "I'm surprised the priests let it happen."

Xander pushed off the wall and steadied himself. "They have little choice. The townspeople may not hold magical abilities, but they do outnumber the priests."

"And the priests are in charge of it, too, down to choosing what everyone can drink, so that makes it their show," Tillit added.

"So a bunch of miraj race in this thing?" I guessed.

"Many dozens in close quarters," Xander replied.

I flinched. "That doesn't sound safe."

Xander nodded. "You are correct. The race is quite dangerous, and many men have died partaking in it."

Tillit slipped his arm over Xander's shoulders and led him down the now-empty street. "The shops first, My Lord. I've got a hunch about this next one. The blacksmith's got a reputation as a bit of a zealot with a hatred for the priesthood."

"A zealot? Shouldn't one of those be *for* the priests?" I wondered.

Tillit shook his head. "Not in this city. A zealot could be for or against the stuffy cloaks, depending on if they benefit from this long occupation or not."

"It is not an occupation," Darda insisted.

We stepped out into a wider street with a few locals gathered against the walls. The sus nodded at them. "You go ask them what they think about the priests."

"Enough," Xander spoke up as he stared straight ahead. "What is done was done many generations ago. Arguing about the consequences only begets worse consequences."

Tillit held up his hands in front of himself. "Don't kill the messenger, My Lord. I was just telling it like it is."

Spiros looked to Xander. "It cannot be ignored."

Xander turned his attention to Tillit. "Where is this next blacksmith shop?"

Tillit looked around us and rubbed his chin. "It should be somewhere-" A scream interrupted him.

The locals and our group looked in the direction of a small shop at an intersection a half a block down. The two sides that faced the perpendicular streets were open with a single support beam holding the roof up.

A woman clad in the simple grayish garb of the citizens stumbled from the shop and pointed behind her. "M-murder! He's been murdered!"

A crowd rushed forward to see the evidence of such a proclamation. Xander led our group down the road to the intersection which by that time was filling with spectators. Tillit and I slipped into the crowd while Spiros with his bulk and Darda with her inexperience were bogged down by the people. We reached the support beam and looked inside. None dared step into the shop for their lying just behind his anvil lay an apron-clad blacksmith. His own hammer was lodged deep into the back of his skull.

I looked around at the shocked faces. "Where's those priest guards when you need them?"

DESERTS OF THE DRAGONS

Tillit swept his eyes over the sandy floor of the shop and pursed his lips. "Maybe closer than you think."

"Step aside! Stand back!" a voice shouted.

The crowd behind us parted for a group of four priest guards. The one in the lead was Captain Benedictus himself, the man who had met us at the gates of the city. He turned to the people and held up his hands. "Stand back!" he shouted.

The crowd shuffled back a half foot. Tillit slipped across the front of the crowd away from the guards and into the shop. Several weapons created by the deceased blacksmith hung from hooks. He grasped a dagger and studied its blade.

Darda came up to me and frowned when she noticed where Tillit stood. "What is that fool-"

"You there!" the captain shouted.

Tillit spun around. His shoulder knocked into the dagger and half a dozen other weapons. They all dropped to the ground in a noisy mess of metal. "Me, sir?"

Captain Benedictus kept his eyes on the sus as he pointed his lance at the crowd. "Get back there!"

Tillit stooped and scooped up the clattering mess of weapons. "My sincerest apologies! Let me clean this mess up first, and I'll be on my way."

"Leave them and rejoin the others!" he demanded.

Tillit grinned and stood. The weapons in his arms clattered to the ground. "Just as you say, captain."

He slipped into the crowd and disappeared around the corner of the shop. I jumped as someone grasped my arm. I whipped my head up to find myself staring into the tense face of Spiros.

"We have to return to the temple," he whispered to me.

I frowned. "Why?"

"It's Xander."

My heart skipped a beat. I whipped my head over my shoulder and looked past Spiros. My dragon lord was nowhere to be seen. Spiros tugged on my arm. "Follow me."

Spiros led Darda and me back through the crowd and out the rear. Xander stood a few yards away. His right shoulder leaned against the wall of a nearby house. He clutched at his chest and his face was scrunched up with pain.

I hurried over and grasped his arm. "What's wrong?"

He shook his head. "It is nothing."

Spiros joined us with Darda behind him. "You are paler than the white sands of Rimal, and that desert is not healthy."

Xander managed a small, trembling smile. "I concede to your wit, Spiros. Let us return to the temple."

"But not without me," Tillit added as he slipped up to us. He glanced over his shoulder and lifted his coat a little. "And this." Inside his overcoat was the dagger he'd inspected.

Darda glared at him. "Return that at once, thief!"

Tillit frowned as he shut his coat. "Yell it where everyone can hear you, will ya?"

"We will discuss this later. Our first priority is to see to Xander," Spiros spoke up.

Xander stood straight, but teetered until he leaned his shoulder against the wall again. "I will not be carried."

"Fine then." I hefted his arm over my shoulders and adjusted his weight. "Then let's get going."

Xander tried to pull free of my grasp. "I am capable pf walking on my own."

I yanked his weight back onto me. "Like hell you can. If you don't want to be carried then get those feet moving."

DESERTS OF THE DRAGONS

With a little help from Spiros-okay, a lot of help-I hefted Xander through the streets and to the bottom of the steep road. The pair of guards met us with unsmiling faces.

Spiros glanced at one of them. "Send a message to Priest Apuleius that his lord is ill and may need his care."

The guard glanced at his companion who frowned, but nodded. The first guard turned to the cage of pigeons and drew one out. He was still scribbling a message as we passed through them and climbed the hill.

Apuleius met us at the top of the long road. At his side was Philo. Our priestly friend set his palm against Xander's chest and looked over the dragon lord's pale face. "You shall have my quarters for the time being, My Lord." He looked up at Spiros and me. "Please bring him this way."

We followed the priest through the white maze and to his room where we set Xander on the wide bed. Apuleius removed the bandages and examined Xander's wound. He pursed his lips and shook his head. "I cannot fathom how, but his wound has not healed."

"Maybe some more of your stuff might help?" I suggested.

He gave a nod. "Perhaps."

We stood by as Apuleius applied more of the salve to Xander's chest. He flinched and gritted his teeth.

Philo turned to our group and smiled. "I hope you enjoyed the festivities in the city."

I nodded. "It was okay until we found the dead guy."

Apuleius paused in his medicating and looked up. "Pardon?"

"It is nothing, Your Holiness. Merely a terrible accident in the blacksmith district," Spiros spoke up.

I looked to Apuleius. "Did you find the book we asked you about?"

He pursed his lips as he capped the salve container and set it on the nightstand beside the bed. "I am afraid not. The book in question appears to be missing."

"I had all the pages search every shelf, but the registry has vanished," Philo confirmed.

Apuleius wiped his hands on a plain towel and turned to us. "Did you meet with the Red Priest?"

I snapped my fingers. "I knew we were missing something. We should go right now."

"I will not allow you to leave without me," he insisted as he tried to sit up.

I set my hands on his shoulders and pressed him back onto the bed. "If Sinbad really is behind this then he's not going to do anything until after the race," I pointed out.

Xander pursed his lips, but looked past me at Spiros. "You will accompany her."

Spiros frowned. "But you are in no condition to-"

"That is an order, captain," Xander commanded him.

His captain narrowed his eyes, but bowed his head. "As you wish."

"My Lord will remain in my care. I will not leave his side until you return," Apuleius assured us.

Tillit smiled as he swept his arm toward the door. "Allow me to lead the way."

The others moved toward the door, but I slipped over to Xander's side. I grasped one of his hands in mine and smiled down at him. "We'll be right back."

He cupped my cheek in his free hand and looked into my eyes. "Be careful."

I snorted. "You know me. I never get into trouble."

A small smile slipped onto his lips as his hand slid down to my Marked shoulder. "If you are, I will know."

CHAPTER 19

I nodded and slipped away to join the others in the hall. We hurried through the palace. I noticed there were the same pages carrying stacks of books, but the boys moved toward the library rather than away.

"Looks like somebody's done reading," I commented.

"The vast armies in the copy shops are very quick," Tillit told me.

We stepped out into the weakening sun of the aging day and crossed the temple grounds. A pigeon flew overhead from somewhere behind us and dove over the hillside into the city. I looked to Tillit. "So I'm guessing the priests use those pigeons to send messages everywhere in the city?"

He nodded. "Yep. There are stations with cages where the birds land, and then a page takes them the rest of the way."

I leaned forward and looked past Tillit at Spiros. "Speaking of messages, why didn't you want to tell Apuleius about that blacksmith?"

"The temple is no longer a safe place to communicate any new information," he pointed out. He quieted for a moment as we strode past the pair of guards and resumed speaking when we had walked into the streets. "We also do not know why he was murdered."

"It might have something to do with this," Tillit commented as he pulled out the stolen dagger.

Spiros took the weapon from him and studied the blade. "It does appear to be the same work as the swords used against us."

Tillit snorted as he was given back the blade. "Of course it is. That's why he was killed. He can't tell us who he sold it to any more than I can get Darda to tell me her age."

Darda straightened and glared at him. "Must you come along?"

He grinned and tapped the side of his nose. "Yep. I'm the only one here who knows where the Red Priest lives."

"You said something about the guards being there," I reminded him.

His eyes flickered to Spiros. "Yeah. Everyone around here wears sandals except those guys. They wear boots to help them ride their hadabs."

Spiros arched an eyebrow. "Footprints?"

Tillit nodded. "Yep. I saw boot tracks in the sand around the body. They're probably messed up by now."

The captain furrowed his brow as he looked ahead. "The guards appeared rather quickly."

"Probably because they were just around the corner after visiting him," Tillit finished.

Darda glared at the pair. "How could either of you suggest such a heinous thing? Temple guards murdering a man? For what purpose?"

Tillit jerked his head in my direction. "Why'd a bunch of monks try to kidnap Miriam and hurt Xander?"

Darda pursed her lips and turned her face away. I looked over at Tillit. "Speaking of monks, is this Red Priest going to slam the door in our face or invite us in for tea?"

He shrugged. "That depends on his mood. Just don't bring up his forced retirement. Losing his comfy position at the temple is still a sore subject for him."

"So just stick to the threatening letter?" I suggested.

"I will make the inquiries," Spiros offered.

Tillit patted his palm against his chest. "I'll do all the talking. He knows me, anyway."

Darda sniffed the air. "What business have you had with him?"

"He may not be an official priest, but he's still got connections in the temple," Tillit pointed out. "That means that any supplies the temple needs, I get them before anybody else knows they need them."

"And what does the fallen priest get in return?" she questioned him.

Tillit shrugged. "A share of the profits, and a little info from me."

Darda started back and gasped. "You would assist a fallen priest in such ways?"

"Reward thine friends and punish thine enemies," Tillit philosophized. He looked around at the street we were in. "Let's see now. He's just around here some-ah, here we are." He stopped us before a nondescript little wood door that was attached to a single floor, mud-dried home. There was only one window to the right of the door, but the wood shutters were closed. Tillit knocked on the door. "Philippus? It's Tillit. I brought some friends to look at your library." The sus paused for a reply. None came. He knocked against. "Philippus? You home?"

Darda rolled her eyes and stepped up beside Tillit. She gave him a push with her hips. "Step aside."

Tillit stumbled to one side as she bent down to peer into the crack between the door and the frame. Darda shook her head. "No one is home."

"You're sure?" Tillit asked her.

She glanced over her shoulder and glared at him. "I have not been a lady-in-waiting all these years to be wrong about whether someone was in their room or not."

Tillit grinned and drew out a large, round chain of keys. Two dozen keys of various sizes jingled on the metal loop. "Good. Now it's my turn."

Darda's jaw dropped open as he moved to the lock on the door and began to try the keys in the hole. "You would enter your friend's home without permission?"

"Yep." One of the keys fit into the lock and he turned it. The door opened and Tillit turned to us with a grin. "Welcome to the home of Philippus."

Darda balled her hands into fists and her body shook as she glared at him. "We cannot enter-" Spiros slipped past her and into the house. She stretched her hand toward him. "Captain Spiros!"

"In such important matters decorum must be set aside," he called from inside.

Darda looked around us. The streets were empty. "But what if we are found."

"Then search quick," Tillit replied as he slipped into the house.

I followed, and Darda reluctantly came in behind me. The home had two rooms. The doorway to the rear room led into a small bedroom. The rest of the house was an open room filled with tables and chairs. The furniture was scattered about the small room, and on top of nearly every surface were stacks of books. Piles of thin books, fat books, short books, and atlas-sized books stretched toward the ceiling. Some of the piles were covered in dust, but most were bare of time's dry indication.

I picked up one of the books and examined its new cover. The other books in the stack were also new. "This guy must really hate old books."

Tillit plucked a book from another stack and opened the cover. He shut the cover and repeated the action for another six books.

Darda glared at him. "Must you be so noisy in your perusal?"

"I'm looking to see which shop made these books," he commented as he continued his searching. "All the copy shops in the city put their stamp in the upper left corner of the inside cover to advertise their business. These don't have one."

"Why wouldn't they?" I wondered.

"Perhaps they did not wish to associate themselves with the fallen priest," Darda suggested.

The only empty space in the room was a small chair beside a table. I took another book and plopped myself down on the seat. My eyes widened and I leapt up.

Spiros looked up from a stack of books and furrowed his brow. "What is the matter?"

DESERTS OF THE DRAGONS

I sidestepped and nodded at the chair. "That seat's still warm."

Spiros set his hand on the hilt of his sword and swept his eyes over the room. "Wait a moment while I inspect the building." He strode into the other room. Darda stepped up to my side while Tillit continued his noisy search. We could see Spiros through the doorway at all times. After a minute he dropped his hand and turned to us. "There is nothing amiss here," he commented as he returned to the main room. He looked around and pursed his lips. "And that is something amiss."

I arched an eyebrow. "Come again?"

"What our enigmatic friend is trying to say is wherever the priest went, he left in a hurry but not after a fight," Tillit explained.

Darda frowned. "How do you know he left in a hurry?"

Tillit nodded at a half-finished cup of drink. "Philippus is very particular about his habits. He may be dirty with his books, but he's clean with his dishes. He always kept them in a cupboard when he wasn't using them and put them back when he was done."

I looked around. There was not a single other dish in sight. "So he left just before we got here because why? He didn't want to talk to us? How'd he even know we were coming?"

"You yourself recognized the method of communication," Spiros commented.

I blinked at him. "Method of-ooh! The pigeon!"

"So why didn't ol' Philippus want to talk to us?" Tillit mused as he picked up another book. He read the cover and wrinkled his nose. "'Dragons, A Tale of Myths.'"

"What did he generally study?" Spiros asked him.

Tillit shrugged and set down the book. "He was always into strange stories about secret treasures and hidden powers of ancient dragons. He was always talking about how the old dragons were more pure and powerful than the ones nowadays. No offense."

Spiros shook his head. "No offense should be taken. It is true that we are not as powerful as our ancestors. Few of us can even change into our full form."

"So how's this ancient dragon stuff fit into what's happening now?" I wondered.

Tillit shrugged. "No idea."

Spiros walked over to the door and half-turned to our small group. "We should return to Xander and inform him of what we found."

CHAPTER 20

Night was nearing when we returned to the temple. In Apuleius's room we found a few more guests. Captain Benedictus stood at Xander's bedside. Behind him stood one of his men. Apuleius was seated at his small table. We walked in partway through the conversation.

"You say you were looking for a specific weapon from the city blacksmiths?" the captain asked Xander.

Xander nodded. "Yes, or rather the lady-in-waiting to my Maiden was curious to see what designs they created in this city." All eyes turned to us as we entered. Xander nodded at Darda. "You may ask her yourself."

The captain's gaze swept over us and stopped on Tillit. His eyes narrowed. "I believe you are the sus who I ordered leave the shop."

Tillit smiled and swept a low bow to the captain. "I am, sir."

"Why did you go into the shop with the dead man laying there?" Benedictus questioned him.

Tillit shrugged. "I didn't hear any arguments from the proprietor."

Benedictus set his hand on the hilt of his short sword. "Do you mean to impede justice, sus?"

The sus folded his arms across his chest and grinned. "Is that what I'm impeding?"

"Captain Benedictus, you must excuse my companion," Xander spoke up. A smile teased the corners of his lips. "My companion is a tradesman like most of his kind and no doubt only wished to inspect the wares before they were impounded by your men."

The captain dropped his sword hand and relaxed his stance, though he still glared at Tillit. "I see. His curiosity may one day lead him to trouble." He turned to Darda. "You are the maid servant who wished to visit the local blacksmith shops?"

Darda bowed her head. "I am."

"Do you swear by all the gods and your ancestors that it was your intention to view the weapons shops?" he questioned her. My heart skipped a beat. I noticed Xander tensed.

Darda nodded. "I swear by my dragon ancestors that that is true, sir."

Benedictus arched an eyebrow, but bowed his head. "Thank you for your honest answer. If you will excuse me, I must find the murderer."

He slipped out of the room and shut the door behind him. Apuleius stood and walked over to Xander's beside. "I feel I must apologize for the captain's questioning. He can be rather direct in his pursuit of justice."

Xander shook his head. "You have no need to apologize. No offense was taken."

I slid up to Darda's side and lowered my voice. "You don't have any dragon ancestors, do you?"

She blushed and lowered her gaze to the floor. "As a human from the other world, no more than yourself, My Lady."

I wrapped my arm around her shoulders and grinned at her. "It's Miriam, Darda. Just Miriam."

"How's the war wound?" I overheard Tillit ask Xander.

My dragon lord set his eyes on me and smiled. "Rather better since you returned." He looked up at Apuleius. "May I have a moment alone with my companions?"

Apuleius bowed his head. "Of course, My Lord. The duties of the temple call me away as it is, but you need merely call when you need me." He slipped out of the hall and gently closed the door behind him.

Xander waited for the door to shut before his eyes flickered to Spiros. "Tell me what has happened, but without being heard."

Spiros walked up to Xander's side and leaned close to his ear. His lips moved, but his voice was so soft even I couldn't hear a whisper. Xander stared straight ahead the whole time and only looked toward Spiros when the captain leaned away.

"You are sure of all your suspicions?" Xander questioned him.

Spiros nodded. "We are."

Xander leaned back against his pillow and frowned. "I see. It is well I sent Apuleius out of the room."

Darda's eyes widened. "You cannot think he-" Xander held up his hand and shook his head.

"I do not believe Apuleius is involved in any way other than his association with the brothers who impede our path to the truth," he assured her.

"So where's this path leading to now?" I asked him as I seated myself on the edge of the bed.

Xander gazed at the sheets that covered him and pursed his lips. "I will accept Sinbad's challenge."

Spiros's eyes widened and he stepped toward the bed. "You intend to race in your condition?"

Xander nodded. "I do. We have no other choice. Our few leads have led to nothing."

Spiros stretched himself to his full height and set his hand on the hilt of his sword. "Allow me to find Sinbad and convince him otherwise."

Xander shook his head. "It would bode ill for us to threaten a member of the most prestigious family among the sands. No, I will race tomorrow, and in so doing I will force Sinbad to tell me what we need to know."

A soft rap sounded on the door. "May we enter?" came the jovial voice of Alzalam.

"Of course, old friend," Xander called out.

The door opened and in stepped Alzalam with his son, Tifl. They both bowed to us before Alzalam hurried over to the bed. He stretched out his arms and took one of Xander's hands in his own.

"I heard of your troubles, old friend, and hurried here as quickly as I could leave my duties," Alzalam told him. He swept his eyes over Xander's pale form and shook his head. "How can I ever be forgiven for failing to protect you?"

DESERTS OF THE DRAGONS

Xander smiled as he shook his head. "This is none of the doing of the thieves. It was merely a case of mistaken identity within the temple."

Alzalam nodded his head. "Good! Good!"

Tifl stepped forward and bowed his head. "Pardon me for asking, but did I hear the name of my most prestigious cousin mentioned before we entered?"

"I was just speaking to my friends about a challenge I have with Sinbad tomorrow at the races," Xander explained. Spiros pressed his lips tight enough together to make them white.

Alzalam started back. "You are sure, my friend? You know as well as I the race is not for the weak of heart or body."

"A night's rest and I will be on my feet," Xander insisted.

Alzalam smiled. "Then I look forward to watching your skill once more. It is a wonderful sight to behold such a fine pair of wings as yours, my friend."

"Have they found out what clan the thieves belonged to?" Tillit spoke up.

The sheikh turned to him and shook his head. "I am afraid not. They may be unaffiliated with any clan for there are many who wander into the desert and find themselves attracted to that sullied life of raiding others for survival."

"Perhaps some day they may be brought under the heal of a strong leader," Tifl commented.

Alzalam chuckled. "Perhaps, my son, but not in my day. Their numbers are too numerous and the desert too large." He turned to Xander. "I am glad to hear no one was harmed, and pray you have a speedy recover. Now if you will excuse me, my son and I have many other friends with whom I must visit, but I will see you tomorrow at the races." The pair bowed to us and left.

Tillit leaned against a wall and whistled. "Now that's a pair."

Spiros turned to him and arched an eyebrow. "How so?"

The sus shrugged. "I just think they know more about what's going on then they're telling, especially when you asked about those thieves."

Darda frowned at him. "How would you have become a purveyor of men?"

He grinned and pushed off the wall. "You don't get in my line of work all these years without learning a trick or two about whether someone's lying or not. Like right now if Spiros told me he wasn't mad at Xander for racing tomorrow, I'd know he was lying."

Spiros pursed his lips. Xander looked over to him. "I understand your concern-" Spiros whipped his head around.

"Do you, *My Lord*? You are as fit to participate in the race as your Maiden, and yet you pretend all is well," Spiros snapped.

Xander leaned forward. His eyes never left those of his captain. "You wish for proof that I am capable of racing tomorrow?"

Spiros stretched himself to his full height and nodded. "I do."

Xander flung the covers over my lap and swung his legs over the side. He eased himself onto his feet and, with one hand on one of the foot posts, he closed his eyes. His face tensed as his wings slowly slid out of his back just above his bandages. Their extreme width meant they reached from one wall of the room to the other and curled at the ends.

Xander relaxed and opened his eyes so they fell on Spiros. "Will that do?"

Spiros pursed his lips, but bowed his head. "It will."

Xander retracted his wings and set himself back on the bed. "Please leave me. I wish to rest until the morrow."

Spiros exited while Darda reluctantly left us. Tillit gave a lazy salute and slipped out after them, closing the door. I remained on the bed and glared at him. "You didn't have to be so mean to Spiros. He's only worried about you."

Xander stretched himself on the bed and leaned his head against my shoulder. He looped one arm around my waist and closed his eyes. "Have I told you how comfortable is your shoulder?"

I sighed. "Not for a long time."

A wisp of a smile slipped onto his lips. "Then let me promise you a long time of peace after we return to Alexandria."

"No Red Dragons or terrifying adventures?" I asked him.

"Nothing but you and me, and the calm waters of the lake," he promised.

"Bringing your wings out took a lot out of you if you're promising me that."

He chuckled. "As perceptive as ever, my Maiden."

I snorted. "A blind man could see it."

"Then I am glad Spiros chooses to be blind."

I pursed my lips as I stroked his hair. "You really think you can do it? The race tomorrow, I mean."

"I. . .will. . .try. . ." His voice drifted off as his breathing evened.

I sighed and shook my head. "I thought I was trouble. . ."

CHAPTER 21

I awoke with a start at the sound of the door creaking open. The early sun of a new day shone through the single window of the spartan room. Apuleius slipped inside with Philo behind him.

"Good morning," Apuleius greeted me.

I shifted atop the bed and winced as my neck cracked. I hadn't dared move for Xander's sake, and his head now lay in my lap. "'morning. . ." I mumbled.

The priest walked over to the bed and shook Xander's shoulder. "My Lord, you must arise soon."

Xander's eyes fluttered open and he eased himself to a seated position. "Is it time?" he wondered as he ran a hand through his messy short hair.

Apuleius nodded. "Yes, or nearly so, My Lord. Breakfast awaits, but your wounds need looking after first."

DESERTS OF THE DRAGONS

I stumbled off the bed as Apuleius went about unwrapping Xander's bandages. Philo slipped up beside me and watched the proceedings. "I hope you slept well."

I nodded. "Like a baby."

"And Our Lord?" he wondered.

I rubbed my sore neck. "Like a log."

He smiled. "Your euphemisms are most amusing, My Lady."

Apuleius finished the unwrapping and bent over the wound. He pressed his fingers gently against the scorched flesh. A smile slipped onto his lips as he straightened and looked at Xander's expectant face. "The wound shows signs of healing."

My heart resumed its normal pace. Philo set a hand on my shoulder. "If you will follow me, My Lady, I will show you to breakfast where your companions await."

I frowned and looked back to Apuleius and Xander. The old priest smiled and nodded. "Philo is quite capable of protecting you against magic, My Lady, and we will join you after I have applied medicine and new bandages."

Philo gestured to the door. "This way, My Lady."

Together we stepped out into the hall and walked the quiet corridors. My thoughts wandered to the coming race and Sinbad's promise. I wasn't so distracted that I missed Philo studying me out of the corners of his eyes.

"Is something wrong?" I asked him.

He meekly smiled and bowed his head to me. "I am sorry, but I could not help admiring your beauty. Your mother must also be very beautiful."

I shook my head. "I wouldn't know. I'm an orphan."

"Surely you know the face of your father," he persisted.

My mind's eye recalled the strange vision of my father and his handsome features. "I didn't know him, either," I replied.

"You must have been quite young to lose them both before you knew their faces," he commented.

"The people who found me thought I was six months old," I told him.

He arched an eyebrow. "Found you?"

I turned my face away and pursed my lips. "I was found in an alley."

He bowed his head. "I feel I must apologize again. It was rude of my to pry into your past."

I smiled and shook my head. "It's fine. I got used to it a long time ago."

Philo chuckled as we stepped out of the main building and onto the grounds. A line of people still stretched out of the temple from the sanctum. "You do not appear to be so old to me. Are you perhaps eighteen?"

I pointed my finger upward. "A little higher."

"Twenty?"

"A little higher."

A crooked smile slipped onto his lips. "Are you perhaps twenty-five?"

I nodded. "Yep, or as close as anyone can guess which means I can lie about it without lying about it."

He chuckled. "You are very full of life, My Lady."

We reached one of the smaller buildings. The smell of fried eggs and greasy meat drifted over us as we stepped through the open pair of doors. Before us was a long hall with rows of tables and benches. Windows on either side allowed fresh light to stream into the room, and at the rear was a long buffet table filled with food. Tillit's wide back stood a the food, and I saw his plate was heaped full of the delicious offerings.

Darda stood up from one of the benches and waved to me. "Miriam!" Opposite her sat Spiros. Both had their plates.

Philo stepped backward and bowed to me. "If you will excuse me, My Lady. As one in charge of the race doctors, I have preparations to make before the competition. Enjoy the food, and I hope to see you later."

I walked alone to the table and took a seat beside Darda. Spiros didn't look up from his plate as he picked away at a smashed pile of chopped potatoes.

Darda looked me over. "Did you sleep well?"

I gave her a smile and a nod. "I'm fine. It's probably just the heat."

Tillit plopped himself at our table with his bulging plate of food. "So how's the stubborn lord this morning?"

I sighed. "He's better."

"Good!" he replied as shoveled the food into a higher pile.

Darda glared at him. "You have no right to eat at the temple when you do not stay within its walls."

He picked up a biscuit and took a huge bite. Bread crumbs flew from his mouth as he spoke. "I was offered a room, I just didn't take it. Besides, isn't it a little early to be arguing?"

"How can you eat at a time like this?" she growled.

He paused and glanced around around at our down-turned faces. "You guys look like somebody died."

"Unlike some people, we have no appetite when our lord is about to get himself killed," Darda snapped at him.

Tillit took another bite and shook his head. "He won't die without a miraj. All the racers have to have their own sand rider, no borrowing, and they have to have it entered before the race. That starts in less than two hours so it's not much time to get himself killed."

Spiros raised his head. Darda relaxed beside me and a small smile teased the corners of her lips. The sun shone brighter than before.

Then all our hopes were dashed.

"All the details have been handled by myself," Apuleius spoke up as he and Xander arrived at the table. Xander stood on his own, but his skin color was still off. "My Lord spoke to me of his desire to race, so I had the brothers repair the minor damage time had done to my own old miraj and enter that in the race under his name."

The gloom over our party returned. We three glared at the sus. Tillit picked up his plate and stood. "I think I'll be going." He slipped away before a murder occurred.

Spiros studied Xander as he took a seat at his side. "You are sure you are well enough to handle the strain?"

Xander smiled back at him. "More than ready."

Spiros sighed and slid his plate in front of his lord. "Then eat and let us be off."

Breakfast was finished and Apuleius led us out of the temple and onto the grounds. The crowd of sanctum-goers was gone. Instead, we heard the far-off roar of the cheering people. We reached the downward slope of the road and looked out over the valley.

Before the high walls of Hadia lay the open desert of Rimal Almawt al'Abyad. Its typically desolate interior was now city unto itself. Tents and hadabs were positioned in

DESERTS OF THE DRAGONS

clumps that stretched from the walls to the bottom of the valley hillside.

The only open space left lay to the northwest where a mile of untouched sand stood. Several dozen miraj were parked close together near two fifty-foot tall wood posts. The posts stood a hundred feet apart, and a line was made in the sand between them.

"We must hurry if we hope to make the lines before the other competitors," Apuleius warned us as he led the way down the road.

I glanced from the road to the festivities and back. "Isn't there an easier way to get there? Like a magic carpet?"

Apuleius paused and turned to me with a smile. "I am afraid not, My Lady, though there have always been rumors of a tunnel once used by the former prince, but it has never been found."

I sighed and followed my companions. "Just my luck to drop into a world of magic that doesn't have a magic carpet."

CHAPTER 22

We walked down the road and through the city. The streets were relatively empty until we reached the main square. The shops were closed and the fountain area was festooned with wildflowers. The citizens danced and laughed in groups. Many waved broad palm leaves over their friends and strangers.

A couple of young women in colorful dresses and bare feet danced over to us. They waved their leaves over us, particularly Xander. My dragon lord smiled and bowed his head to avoid the leaves. The beautiful women giggled and pranced away.

I crossed my arms and glared at him. "Feeling better?"

He looped his arm around my waist and pressed me against his side. "A night's rest beside a lovely woman assisted my recuperation."

DESERTS OF THE DRAGONS

I couldn't help but smile. "Nice save."

We walked to the gate and found the guards had been increased to a dozen men. Benedictus himself was among the patrol. He stepped out of the group of armed men and bowed to us. "Good morning, Your Holiness. Your Lordship, I hope your race goes well this fine day."

I arched an eyebrow. "How'd you know he was going to race?"

"The brothers manage the records of the races, and being a guard for them means I am kept privy to the most pertinent information," he explained.

"Has there been any indication the threat to my brothers will be carried out?" Apuleius asked him.

Benedictus shook his head. "No, Your Holiness, but the day is still young. In the face of such danger I advised Brother Philo to personally choose the brothers who would assist with the race. They are prepared should something go amiss."

Apuleius smiled and nodded. "That is good news. I hope your precautions are not used." He turned to us and gestured to the gate. "Let us proceed to the miraj."

"A moment, Your Holiness," Benedictus spoke up. He nodded at Xander's sword. "Is it wise for His Lordship to carry a weapon during the race? It may throw off his balance or unnecessarily worry the other contestants."

Xander smiled. "My balance would not be effected, but I see your point." He turned to Spiros and unbuckled the sheath and sword from his waist. "If you would hold Bucephalus for a moment." Spiros pursed his lips, but took the weapon.

We followed Apuleius through the gates and out to the open northwest. Being so close to the course, I was able to see that large rocks had been placed in a large circle according to the outer post. The miraj ships were positioned in rows and columns, and at each of their fronts there was attached a fiber rope thirty feet long. Long rows of shirtless muscular men stood beside the ropes ready to pull the ships to the starting line between the posts.

Xander held me closer. "Your eyes wander, my Maiden."

I sheepishly grinned and shrugged. "Can't blame a girl for looking."

Apuleius led us to a large miraj. The green-blue color of the sail stood out among the yellow sand and the other off-white sails.

Apuleius stopped before the vessel and turned to us with a smile. "I thought perhaps My Lord would prefer his colors on the sail."

Xander smiled and stepped onto the ship. "I appreciate your kindness, Apuleius, and could not have asked for a better ship."

I climbed aboard and grasped a rope so I could lean out over the sand and looked around at the competition. One particular miraj caught my attention. A thick crowd of burly men surrounded the ship, and the familiar faces of Sinbad and his horn-blowing henchman stood out aboard the vessel.

I turned to Xander. "I see-" I frowned. Xander stood beside the post with one hand on the wood. He leaned forward and his breathing was quick and shallow. I stepped over to him and set my hand on his shoulder. "You okay?"

He stood straight and smiled at me. "I am."

I frowned as I looked at his pale face. "You don't look okay."

"The heat is very severe today," he commented.

DESERTS OF THE DRAGONS

"I will have some water fetched," Apuleius spoke up. He hurried away and hurried over to a group of gray-cloaked men who stood around a covered cart. Six hadabs were hitched to the cart and a driver sat at the ready. A long table was set up in front of the brothers with barrels of what I guessed was water behind them.

I leaned toward Xander and lowered my voice to a whisper. "You sure you're up for this?"

He looked up at Sinbad. Our foe stared back at us and smirked. "I must be."

Apuleius spoke with Philo, who stood just behind the table, and the brother handed Apuleius a cup. He returned to us with the cup full of water and passed it on to Xander. "A refreshing drink from the well of the sanctum itself, My Lord."

I wrinkled my nose as Xander drank the cup dry. "You can drink that? Isn't it supposed to be holy or something?"

Apuleius nodded as he received back the cup. "It is, and that is why only the drivers of the miraj are allowed to have a drink."

A man with a horn in hand stepped up to the interior post at the starting line. He lifted the instrument and blew a hearty trump that echoed over the valley.

Apuleius offered me his hand. "The miraj must be set at the starting line, My Lady."

I took his hand and let him help me down, but one last glance over my shoulder made my heart sink. Xander looked worse than ever as he stood with one shoulder leaning against the post. Apuleius led us away as the men at the ropes picked them up and placed them on their shoulders. They dug their feet into the sands and stepped forward in time.

Slowly the miraj with their smooth skids slid across the sands. The crowds in the tents, heeding to the call of the horn, flowed out to the course. The people stopped just outside the ring of stones and created a line that marked the outer border of the course. One part of the border at the finish line was surrounded by larger stones and none in the crowd save for a dozen people stepped within the square. Alzalam was among them with Wahid at his side, but Tifl was nowhere to be seen.

Apuleius took my arm and gestured to the square. "This way, My Lady. Those who own a miraj are allowed a spot at the finish line."

"But we don't own it," I pointed out.

He pressed a finger to his smiling lips and lowered his voice to a whisper. "That is not how anyone else knows it, My Lady."

Apuleius led our small group into the square, and Alzalam turned to us and bowed. "My friends! What a pleasure to see you on this glorious day! I am glad to see His Lordship is well enough to race against my nephew. It will be a sight to behold."

"Is your son not joining us, good sheikh?" Apuleius asked him.

Alzalam shook his head. "No. He dares not come among so many revelers for fear of the wine."

I stepped up to the start line side and looked out over the sea of masts among the desert. The ships were positioned twelve columns along the starting line and two rows deep. Xander stood at the ready with his ropes in hand and his ship positioned at the outer rear. Sinbad was placed in the front against the inner post.

"Why's he in the back?" I asked our group.

DESERTS OF THE DRAGONS

"He was a late entry, My Lady, and thus was placed in the rear," Apuleius explained.

The man with the horn blew his instrument again and tow men moved off the field. The sailors of each miraj stretched out their short, thick wings. All except my dragon lord who was the last to reveal his long wings.

"Damn it. . ." I heard Spiros mutter as he stepped forward.

Apuleius set his hand on the captain's shoulder and shook his head. "The wheels have been set in motion. You cannot interfere with Our Lord's choice."

My heart thumped louder as the crowd quieted. The horn blower blew again. Everyone's head turned to the left. I followed their gaze.

In the distance came the familiar haze of a coming naqia dust storm. The wall of sand stretched for half a mile and rose into the sky some two hundred feet. The ground trembled with the thunder of the unicorn hooves as they sped our way. The crowd, once joyous, shrank from the coming storm. The distance between us and it shrank to a hundred yards. Darda grabbed my arm and tensed beside me.

The horn blower took a deep breath and blew his instrument good and loud. The sound reverberated the air and pained my ears. The storm veered off to the right of the course and behind the crowds, but the magical winds continued on their path forward into the sails of the miraj. That meant that for a brief moment the crowd was trapped between the whipping winds behind us and the echoes of its fury in front of us.

Darda gasped and wrapped herself around me. I hugged her tight as the sails billowed and the miraj leapt forward. The race had begun.

All the miraj were given the same amount of air, but the skill of the drivers was what shone out as they broke out of the starting line. Sinbad took an early lead as he rushed ahead of the pack and took the first corner close to the rocks. Others followed close behind, but my attention was riveted on that green-blue sail.

Xander was stuck on the outside track and forced to go around the slower of his competitors. He didn't get a chance to break to the middle until the straight stretch on the opposite side of the course. At the second corner there were still a dozen miraj ahead of him, and there was nearly half a lap between him and Sinbad.

The miraj rushed by with such force that I felt myself physically drawn toward the course. Several of the crowds, packed as they were close to the rocks, screamed and shoved as those in front regretted their wonderful view.

Xander swept past with his wings close by his back and a pained look on his face. I looked to my companions. "How many of these do they do?"

"Four," Apuleius told me.

I turned back to the race. Xander passed another four ships, but the strength of the magic alone couldn't get him to close the gap. He was stuck in eighth for another lap before he opened his wings wide and flapped them. The power of his own wind forced his miraj off the ground. It hit that sands at nearly double the speed.

"Too soon. . ." I heard Spiros murmur.

"What do you mean?" I asked him.

Spiros shook his head. "His body is in no condition to for a full lap, much less for the lap and a half that remains."

DESERTS OF THE DRAGONS

Xander reached the corner without slowing and his ship teetered on the brink of flipping over. He yanked on his ropes and leaned toward the elevated side. A gasp arose from the crowd as the tip of his wing ground itself into the sands. It became an anchor and a rudder, allowing him to turn at that sharp angle and fast speed. He reached the straight and his miraj landed back on both skids. The crowd blew up in applause and whistles as he sped past us.

Only one lap remained, but Xander was back in the race. His competitors fell beneath the strength of his wings and soon only he and Sinbad remained. Xander reached the far-off straight with only fifty feet between him and Sinbad. The cocky young dragon looked over his shoulder as Xander pushed his wings to flap faster. They were nearly neck-and-neck. The final corner was coming up.

Then it all went wrong.

CHAPTER 23

Xander reached the corner on the outside of Sinbad, but when he tried to dragon his wing the tip shriveled back. He fell onto one knee and clutched the ropes as the entirety of his wings disappeared into his back. The miraj teetered on one skid and the billowing sail dragged the ship off the course. The crowds behind the rocks screamed and scattered as the ship plowed through.

The miraj hit one of the large stones and tipped over. Xander was thrown and landed hard on the sand where he rolled for several yards. He came to a stop face-down and lay still.

"Xander!" I shouted as I rushed forward.

Spiros sprinted past me, as did Apuleius. They reached Xander as the crowd began to gather around my fallen dragon lord. Together they gently rolled him onto his back and Apuleius laid his head against Xander's chest.

Darda grabbed my arm ten feet from where Xander lay and stopped me. "It would be better if you remained here, My Lady," she warned me.

"Let me go!" I wrenched myself from her grasp and slid over to Xander's side. Xander lay still. I looked at Spiros and Apuleius. "Is he-?"

Apuleius pursed his lips and shook his head. "No, but he is gravely ill. I cannot think what would force his wings to disappear before he lost consciousness."

"I can," Spiros spoke up. He lifted his eyes to mine. "Dragon's Bane would force him to his human form."

My eyes widened. Darda came up to us and furrowed her brow. "But a dragon must come into contact with the Bane to feel its effects."

By this time the crowds pressed close around us. The gray-cloaked brothers pushed their way through the crowd toward us. "Please step aside!" Philo called to the tight mass of dragon kind that surrounded us.

The crowd tried to back up, but the front group crashed into the rear guard. The whole mess of people flowed like a pulsating heart back and forth against and away from us. At each tight push of dragons against me I felt as though the air was knocked out of me.

Spiros drew his sword and held it high into the air. Its sharp blade glistened in the bright light. "Move back!" he shouted.

The weapon gave the crowd as a whole incentive to step back, and the white-cloaked men reached us. They positioned themselves at the four points around Xander's prone body, and Philo moved to his side. He pressed his hand against Xander's chest. My dragon lord winced and his teeth ground together.

Philo looked up at our small group, most especially Apuleius. "We must return him to the temple."

"I will forge you a path," Spiros offered as he brandished his weapon in the direction of the wagon.

Spiros broke a path through the crowd. Four of the brothers lifted Xander between them and carried him along the open path.

A cheer arose from the farther, and some of them flowed toward the course. I looked back over my shoulder and saw Sinbad slide to a stop past the finish line. He leapt off his miraj and strode toward us. The crowd full of congratulations slowed him down, but didn't stop him as he closed the gap between us.

"Spiros!" I shouted as I pointed in Sinbad's direction.

Spiros followed my finger and pursed his lips together. He turned and allowed the brothers and our group to pass him. He dropped his hand on my shoulder and leaned toward me. "I will guard the rear. See that Xander is taken care of."

I nodded. "I promise."

I hurried to catch up to the quick brothers as they pushed their way the final yards to the waiting cart. Apuleius was just behind them and Darda was near my side when a shout echoed over the yelling and cheering.

"Bandits!"

The cry came from somewhere in the crowd. A great clamor arose from the spectators as they shouted and screamed. Many tried to flee in all directions, leading to a panic that quickly escalated into a stampede.

DESERTS OF THE DRAGONS

"Miriam!" Darda shouted as she was pulled away from me.

I reached for her outstretched hand, but missed it by an inch. A pair of strong hands grabbed my upper arms. I whipped my head around and found myself staring into Philo's tense face.

"Please come with me, My Lady," he instructed me.

He gripped me tight as he led me through the rough, panicked crowds. I watched as Apuleius was also pulled away by the tide of people. Xander was lifted into the covered cart a moment before we reached the vehicle. Philo helped me inside where two of the brothers sat on either side of Xander.

Philo pulled himself into the vehicle beside me and looked ahead at the driver. "Hurry!"

The driver cracked a whip above the heads of the hadabs. The creatures howled and rushed forward through the crowds. The people leapt out of the path of the wild beasts as the cart rocked back and forth.

Xander winced and ground his teeth together. His breathing was quick and shallow. I grasped one of his hands that lay on his chest. It trembled in mine.

A slight clucking noise caught my attention. I looked up and found Philo shaking his head as he looked down at Xander. "Such a noble man to be brought down so low by Dragon's Bane."

My heart skipped a beat as my own hands began to tremble. I swallowed a lump in my throat. "H-how do you know it's Dragon's Bane?"

He raised his head and smiled at me. "Because I am the one who administered the unique substance."

"Y-you?" I stuttered.

"You seem very excited, My Lady. Perhaps a rest would do you some benefit." He glanced to my left and nodded.

I whipped my head in that direction just as the brother wrapped his arm around me. He pulled me against him and pressed a wet cloth over my nose. A pungent odor invaded my nostrils. The world around me began to spin.

The last view I had was of the walls of the city as we passed far around the gate to the rear. Then the world turned black.

CHAPTER 24

A loud clanging noise awoke me. My mind felt like it was trapped in a heavy fog. I shook off the lethargy and creaked opened my eyes. A harsh bright light made me blink, but I soon adjusted to the glare. What I couldn't adjust to was the surprise.

I was seated against a stone wall in a small, circular room. The floor was also stone, and an ancient wooden door with a peephole slit also bespoke of the normal conditions of my new world. What wasn't normal was the single light bulb that hung from the curved stone ceiling above me. Its light blinked often, but there definitely a flow of electricity into its interior. The wire itself came into the room through a small hole in the wall above the door.

"I thought you would never awaken."

I whipped my head to my left. Xander was leaned against the wall a foot from me. He gave me a weak smile. "You are quite a heavy sleeper."

"Xander!" I tried to lunge at him, but my arms and legs were bound by chains. The chains ran from my body to the wall to my right. I shifted and the clanging noise from before came from my ankles as the chains dragged across the hard floor.

Xander was likewise bound, but he scooted over so we nearly touched. "Are you unharmed?"

My eyebrows shot up. "Am I unharmed? You're the one who collapsed mid-race."

He pursed his lips and stared ahead. "Is that what happened? I can hardly recall anything but the harsh pain."

"You lost your wings and control of the miraj," I told him.

"Did I harm anyone?"

I shook my head. "No, but seriously, how are *you* feeling?"

He shifted and winced. "Very much like a human."

My face fell. "What's wrong with that?"

"If we wish to escape I must be something more."

I looked around at our less-than-posh surroundings. "Any idea where we even are? This doesn't look like the temple."

He shook his head. "I cannot begin to fathom this area, nor even this source of light."

I nodded up at the bulb. "That's electricity."

Xander tilted his head to one side and studied the bulb with wide eyes. "Electricity has a strange form."

"That's just the light bulb. It used electricity to make that light," I explained.

Footsteps beyond the door caught our attention. They rang down a hollow hall and stopped before the door. There was the sound of a key in the lock, and the entrance swung open.

Philo stepped into the room and stopped beneath the ugly light. Shadows deepened the wide smile on his face as he bowed to us. "Good evening, My Lord. My Lady. I hope you both slept well."

I glared at him. "Not as well as you are when I get a hold of your scrawny neck."

He straightened and clucked his tongue. "Such language from a Maiden of the great city of Alexandria." His eyes flickered to Xander. "But then, I had heard your predecessor also had a sharp tongue."

Xander narrowed his eyes. "From whom did you learn that?"

"From the great Red Lord, of course. It is to he and he alone that we owe our allegiance," Philo told us.

I curled my lips up at him. "Typical. You bad guys always have to gang up on the good guys."

Philo returned his attention to me. He bent down on one knee before me and his eyes studied my face. "Those are strange words coming from the daughter of a 'bad guy,' as you call us."

I frowned. "You don't know my parents."

He chuckled. "It is true I did not know your parents, but I knew your father quite well." I started back. He nodded. "Yes. As you suspected, he was once a brother in this temple, and was deeply engrossed in serving our lord the Red Dragon."

My eyebrows crashed down as I glared at him. "You're lying."

He sighed. "I thought perhaps you would not believe me, so I procured this from the library." He drew a large tome from his robe and placed it in front of me. The cover told me it was the missing brother registry. Philo opened the book to a particular page and tapped his finger on one of the lines. "Here is your father's own signature."

I looked over the line. The name read Mark Pryor. The first name was later crossed through and replaced with Marcus.

"He held on to his original name for only a short while before His Holiness Philippus changed it to a more suitable form for this world," Philo told me.

I lifted my head and frowned. "'This world?'"

He nodded. "Yes. You see, your father being here was a complete accident. He wandered through one of our test portals which we thought had failed and came from your world to our own."

My eyes widened. "Then he was-"

"Human? Undoubtedly, but with a gift of magic that our world granted him," Philo confirmed as he tucked the book back into his robe. "That is why he proved to be such a useful ally when it came to creating more portals."

"You would open more portals and destroy both our worlds merely for electricity?" Xander challenged him.

Philo glared at him with his single eye. "How naive of you to believe such a fairy tale. As anyone who is not ignorant of the theories would know, the portals are a way to save our world. However, I have not come here to argue with you. Rather-" he returned his attention to me and smiled, "-I have come here to confirm the suspicions I have of your beautiful Maiden. I thought perhaps she would join us as her father did."

"None of this proves he was with you," I snapped.

"Oh, but it does." Philo reached into his robe and pulled out a faded piece of rolled up parchment. He opened the parchment and showed me the contents.

The document was an oath to the Red Dragon. At the bottom was a signature signed in blood. It was my father's name and the exact same signature as that in the registry. My heart sank. My mind swirled with questions that I couldn't form into words.

"Do you not see now that I speak the truth? Your father was a loyal subject of the Red Dragon till his dying day."

I whipped my head up and glared at him. "'Until his dying day?' Was the same day he stopped following him the day you killed him?"

Philo sighed and climbed to his feet. "You certainly have your father's stubbornness, but perhaps your mind might be changed in good time."

There came a knock on the door. "Enter," Philo called.

A man clad in a red robe stepped inside and bowed to the traitor. "My apologies for disturbing you, sir, but there is a problem with the latest portal."

Philo frowned. "What sort of problem?"

"It is too large to be stable."

Philo sighed and turned his attention back to us. "It appears duty calls me away, but it is probably for the best. I am afraid I have little authority over your fate. That is up to the Agent of the Red Dragon assigned to this area, and he will be here shortly. While you await him, feel free to ask the guard for anything you need."

"I'd like to get out of here," I quipped.

He chuckled. "Within reason, that is. Farewell."

He walked out into the hall with the red-robed figure and the door shut behind him. There was a clang as the door was locked.

"Have the arrangements been made for the agent and his particular drinking habits?" I heard Philo ask someone.

"Yes, sir."

"Then let us see to this portal." Their footsteps retreated down the corridor.

I sank down against the wall behind me and hung my head. My mixed thoughts swirled in my head. Some of them came out as whispered words. "Was he really a traitor. . .?"

"Do not believe any of what the Red Dragon followers tell you," Xander warned me.

I lifted my head and glared at him. "Did you see the signatures? They were the same."

He pursed his lips as he studied me. "Perhaps your father was once seduced by the followers of the Red Dragon, but as you said, he was murdered, and by those whom he most trusted. That points to him not being like them, and perhaps being antithetical to their beliefs."

My chains rattled as I slumped down and stared at the floor. "Maybe, but I don't think we're going to be able to find out."

Xander looked around at our surroundings. "That is true. Whoever this agent is of the deceased Red Dragon, they will not show us any mercy."

I winced. "Yeah. You did kind of kill their lord, didn't you?"

He nodded. "That is true."

I sighed and swept my eyes over the room. "If only there was a puddle in here, or maybe a-" My eyes lit up as an idea hit me. I sat up and looked at the door. "Hey! You out there!" I called.

"Miriam!" Xander hissed.

The board slid open and a gray-clad guard looked through the hole. "What do you want?"

"Could I get some water? I'm dying of thirst here."

He rolled his eyes. "Very well, but only one drink." He shut the peephole and in a few moments the door was opened. The guard stepped inside with a tin cup in one hand. With the better view of his person I was able to see he wasn't dressed as a brother, but as a temple guard. He stooped in front of me and tipped the cup toward me. "Drink deeply for I will not allow you another chance."

I took a deep breath and let the water from the large cup flow into my mouth. The guard poured it all in and lowered the cup. "Satisfied?"

I smiled and nodded. He stood and left us, locking the door behind him.

Xander looked from the entrance to me. "What do you-" he blinked at me as he noticed my bulging cheeks. "Are you well?"

I tilted my head back and opened my mouth. A long water dragon the size of a small snake drifted out. The creature arced downward and slipped into the chain lock that held my feet. The dragon wiggled around for a few moments before I heard an undeniable 'click.' The lock popped open and the dragon slithered out with a big grin on its small face.

I twisted around and nodded at the lock that bound my wrists. The dragon slithered behind me and freed that lock, as well. I scurried over to Xander, and in a few moments we were both free.

Xander tried to stand, but his legs gave out and he dropped back to the floor. I slipped in front of him and pressed a finger to my lips. The dragon hissed at him. I knocked it upside its wet head. The dragon shrank back.

I turned and crept over to the entrance where I knelt down to the space between the door and the floor. The dragon slipped underneath the door. A few moments later I heard a muffled cry followed by something heavy slamming against the door. The entrance swung open and the guard dropped backward into the room where he landed with a thud on his back. There was a nice goose egg growing on the back of his head. My dragon snake slipped off of him and curled around me. I returned to Xander and draped one of his arms over my shoulders.

I took a deep breath through my nose and together the three of us shuffled from the room. We stepped out into the hall and I looked to our left.

"Halt!" a voice shouted.

I whipped my head to my right. A crowd of guards stood twenty yards away. In their center stood the red dragon whom we had met at the island of Ui Breasail. His red sash stood out against the gray robed figures around him. Beside him was a wizened old man with a three-foot long gray beard and draped in red robes.

I gulped. Like an open drain, my little dragon disappeared into my mouth. "Oh shit," I muttered.

The red dragon grinned at us. "Capture them again," he commanded the gray cloaks.

I turned and sped down the hall as fast as Xander's weak legs would take us. The heavy footsteps of the gray-cloaked temple guards pounded behind us. Each step we took they made three.

DESERTS OF THE DRAGONS

We turned a corner and I noticed a door on our right that was ajar. I slammed my shoulder into it and we stumbled into a room hardly larger than our former cell. Against one wall was a large, swirling portal. Before it stood Philo and the red-clad priest. They both turned at our barging entrance and gawked at us.

Between the mysterious portal and the clamor of swords behind us, I steamed full speed ahead. We rushed past the shocked Philo and his companion, and lunged into the unknown. One last, lingering thought hit me as we leapt into the void.

I wish I was home.

CHAPTER 25

The familiar warm pool of liquid wrapped around me like a spongy blanket. I shut my eyes to keep out the warped gray liquid. Like the last time I traveled through one of the portals, the pressure was nearly unbearable. Only Xander's hand in mine kept me from panicking.

Our tense ride ended with a hard stop as we were thrown out of the portal and onto hard ground. The portal shut behind us with a soft clap and we were plunged into the darkness of night.

I sat up and groaned. "Remind me not to do that again."

There wasn't a reply to my unoriginal joke. I looked around. The portal had dropped us in a clearing surrounded by a thick forest. The clear night sky allowed the stars to shine their lights on the thickly carpeted ground. A dark shadow lay a couple feet from me.

"Xander!" I shouted as I scrambled on my hands and knees over to him.

Xander lay face-down in the pine needles. I rolled him over and looked him over. His eyes flickered open and focused on me. "Miriam," he whispered.

I smiled back at him. "You really need to lose some weight."

He weakly chuckled and winced. "Perhaps when we return to Alexandria."

I glanced around at our wooded surroundings. "*If* we ever get back to Alexandria. I have no idea where we-" My eyes fell on an opening in front of us. A gasp escaped my lips.

Xander furrowed his brow as I sat him up and stood. "Miriam?"

I walked to the edge of the clearing where the ground sloped downward and looked out on a mass of twinkling lights. Spread out before us in a low river valley was the city of my childhood. A soft breeze flew from the city and the smell of industrialization wafted into my nostrils.

I shook my head. "I'm. . .home?"

A shuffling behind me caught my attention. I turned to find Xander coming up to my side. "If I'm home, how did you get through the portal without-you know-being evaporated?"

He clasped my hand in his. "I would venture to say our connection is what saved me from destruction." He set his hand against a nearby tree and looked out on the sparkling view. "So this is your home?"

I shrugged. "Well, used to be. It's where I grew up."

He turned to me. "You grew up among the stars?"

I laughed and shook my head. "No. Those are like that light we saw in the cell, only a lot more."

His eyes widened and he returned his attention back to the city. "Is there so much electricity that every person might have one of these 'light bulbs?'"

I covered my face to stifle my snort before I cleared my throat. "Definitely, and the rich have up to three."

"I would like to see this wondrous city," he requested.

I glanced around at the woods. "I don't think we have much of a choice. The portal disappeared, and unless you know how to open a portal then we'll have to get back to our world through the-" The bright light of the portal reopened. "Or maybe not." Gray-clad figures stepped out of the swirling mass. "Or maybe yes!"

I grabbed Xander's hand and dragged him down the slope toward the city. Shouts came from behind us, and more illuminated woods on either side told me there was an invasion force of monks through a half dozen new portals.

"These guys really don't care about the fabric of space!" I quipped.

Xander couldn't reply. His breathing was labored and he stumbled over every rock and root. One particularly vindictive root caught his foot and sent him tumbling into me. Together we rolled forward down the hill and into a thicket of brush. The sharp branches caught us in their unforgiving grasp and stopped our tumbling.

I wrestled myself free of the brambles and found Xander hopelessly thrashing among his own branches. I forded my way over to him, but paused when lights above us caught my attention. They were the beams of flashlights

DESERTS OF THE DRAGONS

carried by our foes, the gray-clad guards of the temple. One of the beams floated toward my dragon lord.

I lunged forward and crashed down atop Xander. He stiffened, but didn't make a noise as I lay atop him. The guards circled our thicket and stopped.

"Where did they go?" one of them muttered.

"Burn the bushes if you must. They could not have gone far," came the familiar voice of Benedictus.

The guards opened their empty hands. Flames burst from their palms and lit up the area. I caught my breath as they began to toss their balls of fire into the brush. The dry bushes burst into flames and cast their light over the whole of the area.

"There! There they are!" one of them shouted as he pointed a finger at us.

I leapt to my feet and dragged Xander with me. We backed up until our backs hit the rough bark of a thick tree. The fire-wielding guards circled us and closed in. My heart thumped loudly in my chest. It skipped a beat when a hand slipped into mine. I looked up into Xander's face. He smiled at me. My face fell as I shook my head.

Not like this.

A green light burst from my pocket. I looked down in bewilderment as the light was followed by a warm, comforting heat. The light made our foes pause. I reached into my pocket and drew out the Soul Stone. It glowed with a beautiful green light that pulsed with heat.

I blinked against the strong light. "What the-" A brilliant flash burst from the stone.

The light flew outward in front of us and stopped a few feet away. The rays of green formed themselves into layers of bands that circled one another until they formed a circle.

The bands melded together and another flash of light signified the completion of their task and the creation of a new portal.

I gaped at the swirling mess of green light. Our foes likewise gawked at the beautiful sight, but only for a moment.

"Capture them!" Benedictus shouted.

They moved in closer. I tightened my hold on Xander's hand and pulled him into the portal.

CHAPTER 26

The trip through the portal wasn't like the others. There was no suffocating liquid or pure darkness. Rather, there was a soft warm glow of blue-green light that washed over me and guided us along the path.

Right until we dropped out of the ceiling and landed hard on a stone floor. Being the leader, I dropped out first. Xander landed atop me and knocked the air from my lungs.

I coughed and tried to crawl out from beneath his weight. "Diet," I wheezed.

"Miriam!" a voice shrieked.

I whipped my head up and found myself staring at the shocked face of Darda. A look around told me we were in our shared room in the Temple. Xander dragged himself off me and stumbled over to the bed where he eased himself onto the edge.

Darda helped me up and looked from me to the weakened dragon lord. "What has happened? How did you come to go through a portal into this room?"

I shook my head. "It's a long story."

"Where is Spiros?" Xander asked his servant.

"Searching for both of you with the brothers," Darda replied.

"Have they caught Philo?" I asked her.

Darda furrowed her brow as she shook her head. "Of course not. Why should he need to be caught?"

My jaw dropped open. "Because he's the one who kidnapped us!"

Darda shook her head. "That cannot be. He informed us that bandits had disguised themselves as his men and stolen you away. He himself only barely managed to escape."

My eyebrows shot down and I balled my hands into fists. "He's a god damn liar! He told me himself he was the one who gave Xander the Dragon's Bane!"

"Miriam, you must be quiet," Xander whispered.

I whipped my head to him. "What?"

"Be quiet or we will be heard by the guards."

I winced. "Oh. Right. Sorry."

Xander pursed his lips as he turned his attention to Darda. "Retrieve him, but without telling the brothers that we are found."

Darda furrowed her brow. "But they need to know-"

"No they don't," I told her.

Darda pursed her lips, but bowed her head before she hurried from the room. I plopped myself on the bed beside Xander and winced as a bruise formed on my hip. I pressed my hand against the growing bump, but there was interference.

I lifted my hand and found myself staring at the Soul Stone. It no longer glowed, and the heat was also gone. I looked up at Xander. "How the hell did that happen, anyway?"

He shook his head. "I cannot be sure, but I would venture to guess the Soul Stone you possess has the ability to create portals."

My face fell. "Perfect. My gift can rip a hole between worlds and doom us both."

Xander tilted his head back and studied the empty ceiling. "Perhaps not. The portal created by the brothers and the one the stone created were very different." He looked back to me. "Were either of those similar to the portal at High Castle?"

I nodded. "Yeah, the first one was pretty much exactly like that one."

"Then we might assume that the one created through the magic of the brothers is more destructive than the one created by your natural portal," he surmised.

"But we can only assume," I pointed out.

He sighed and nodded. "That is-" The door flew open and Spiros rushed in with Darda close behind him. Xander's sheath with Bucephalus swung against his left hip.

Spiros strode over to us and dropped on one knee before Xander. He bowed his head. "I am sorry, My Lord. I have failed in protecting either you or your Maiden."

Xander smiled and shook his head. "You cannot be blamed. Our foes are numerous and cunning. Their deceit hidden behind their gray robes gave them the greater advantage."

Darda stepped up beside Spiros and clasped her hands in front of her. "Then the brothers-?"

"Some of them are our enemies, but we do not know their true numbers," Xander confirmed.

Spiros lifted his head and frowned. "The brothers, My Lord?"

Xander nodded. "It was they and the temple guards who kidnapped us, and being as we are in the temple we have not escaped their grasp."

"But where *is* safe?" I wondered.

"The oasis of Alzalam, or perhaps Almukhafar," Xander suggested.

I frowned. "That sounds like running away."

Spiros stood and smiled. "A strategic retreat is never foolish."

The sound of many feet outside the room warned us of a coming problem. Spiros spun around and unsheathed both of the swords he wore. Darda drew out four of her smaller daggers and held them between her fingers.

Xander stood on his shaky feet. "No. You cannot win against their magic."

Spiros looked over his shoulder and grinned. "Now that we know our enemy I can remind you why you honored me with the position of captain of Alexandria."

The door burst open and slammed into the opposite wall. The fire-wielding guards and brothers, their faces covered by their hoods, stormed inside, but the narrow doorway only allowed them to enter one at a time. Spiros raised his sword and, with a great roar, charged at them.

The intruders threw their fireballs, but Spiros deflected them with the broad sides of his swords. The flames heated the metal to where they burst into flames. He reached the first one and cut him down with the red-hot weapon. The man screamed and fell to the floor.

DESERTS OF THE DRAGONS

The others behind him tried to spread out, but Darda threw her daggers. The blades sank deep into their chests and they joined their brother on the floor. The incoming brothers tried to back up, but the greater numbers at the rear forced them into Spiros's flaming sword. Together Spiros and Darda dealt with the two dozen who dared tried to enter.

Spiros leapt into the hall and cut another down. The final brother turned tail and fled down the corridor. Darda and I helped Xander out into the hall.

Spiros turned to us as the flames died down on his blade. He was covered in sweat and blood, but he merely sheathed his sword and held out Bucephalus. "I am sorry to have ruined this blade against so cowardice a foe."

Xander smiled as he took his sword and sheath back. "That was an impressive reminder of your skills."

A noise made me I glance down the hall. My eyes widened as they fell on another two dozen gray-clad brothers, and the width of the hall didn't give us any advantage. "Um, compliments later, running now!"

"Forgive me, Xander." Spiros sheathed his sword and swept Xander into his arms. "But you are too weak to outrun them." He rushed down the hall in the direction of the entrance.

Darda grabbed my hand and tugged me along behind them. "And I will watch over you!"

We four ran down the hall with the brothers close behind. Fireballs shot over our heads. "Halt!" yelled one of the brothers.

"Halt yourself!" I shouted back.

Our feet echoed down the marble halls as the walls were scorched by fire. Spiros ran into the intersection that led in the direction of the sanctum or the entrance. Darda and I followed, and I looked to our right at the entrance. The pair of doors were shut, and a half dozen brothers stood facing us. Their menacing presences and hidden faces told me they wouldn't open the doors, even if we said 'please.'

"How many of these guys are there?" I growled.

"Far too many," Spiros replied as he stepped back.

I glanced over my shoulder. Our tailing group was only a few yards back. I whipped my head to our left. The doors to the sanctum were also shut, but they weren't blocked.

"Into the sanctum!" I shouted.

"But we will be trapped!" Darda pointed out.

"I have a plan!" I insisted

We turned left and ran up to the sanctum entrance. Spiros slammed his shoulder into one of the doors. The door gave way enough for us to slip through. Spiros set Xander down on his unsteady legs before he pressed his shoulder against the inside of the door. Darda joined him, and together the pair shut the door.

It wasn't a moment too soon. Our pursuers pounded their fists against the door, and many of them pushed against it. Darda and Spiros dug their heels into the slick floor and leaned their backs against the door. Xander joined them and put his weight into holding the entrance.

"We cannot hold for long!" Spiros yelled.

I looked to my left at the calm pool. The blue light from the water reflected off the walls. I pursed my lips and marched up to the water.

"Hey! Is there anyone home!" I shouted.

"Miriam, what are you doing?" Darda questioned me.

I looked over my shoulder at my friends. "I'm trying to get the fae's attention."

She frowned. "*That* is your plan?"

I shrugged. "It's worth a-" A soft twinkle of water caught my attention.

I turned back and gasped. An inch from my nose was the face of a beautiful young woman. I stumbled back and took in the full view of the glowing blue fae. She appeared to be thirty with a slim figure blue skin like those of the other celestials. Her attire was a soft blue imitation of the plain, low cut dresses worn by the women of the desert. Her long blue hair was braided and intertwined with the reddish desert flowers of the oasis.

"Alihat Dhahabia. . ." I whispered.

She drew back and smiled at me. "My greetings to you as well, young Estelwen. It has been a long time since we spoke. I am glad to see you well and grown."

I blinked at her. "You know me?"

She nodded. "Yes. Your father used to bring you here quite often. He thought it would comfort you in the absence of your mother."

"Then you knew my father?" I asked her.

"Yes. He was a gentle man who felt very keenly about his adopted world," she told me.

I frowned. "Then why did he try to destroy it by helping the Red Dragon?"

She shook her head. "He was led astray as many men by the promise of a better world."

The pounding behind me grew louder. I swallowed the lump in my throat. "I really want to know more, but I've got to get my friends out of here first. Is there any way you can help us?"

Alihat floated down to me and cupped one of my cheeks in her palm. Her touch was nearly as warm as the desert, but soft like a cool breeze. "You do not need my help, little niece. You yourself hold the power you seek."

I frowned and shook my head. "I don't understand. You mean I need to use your water?"

Her eyes drifted down to my pocket. "Use your gifts, and the truth shall be open to you."

She drew away as I pulled out the Soul Stone. The smooth surface reflected my puzzled face. "But I don't-" I raised my head, but the woman was gone. "Hey!" I rushed to the edge of the pool and looked into the empty waters. "Come back! How do I use this thing? Where's the on switch?"

"Miriam!" Darda shouted.

A large thump slammed into the door. I spun around and found the faces of all my friends staring at me. The door behind them bulged as the invaders thumped against its surface.

I raised the Soul Stone and looked into its shimmering surface. The green glass reflected my stern expression. I took a deep breath and closed my eyes as I clasped the stone in both my hands. "Please open a portal to somewhere safe so I can save my friends."

The same brilliant green light as before burst from the Soul Stone. It twined itself into a portal that stood between me and my friends.

The door burst open. My friends stumbled back as our enemies rushed inside. The lead gray-cloak threw off their hood and revealed himself as Philo. He gaped at the swirling green-blue portal. "By all the gods. . ."

"Get in the portal!" I shouted to my companions.

Darda turned around and rushed into the light.

Xander stumbled toward me. "Not without you!"

"You'll reward me later!" Spiros shouted as he threw one of Xander's arms over his shoulders and pulled them both into the portal.

That left only me. I took a step toward the portal.

"Miriam!"

I paused and looked across the portal. It was Philo who called to me. He stretched out his hand and smiled at me. "Join us, like your father before you."

I glared at him. "Hell no."

Then I threw myself into my portal.

CHAPTER 27

I was prepared for the soft touch of green-blue light. What I got was a push into an unfamiliar room. One moment I was in the sanctum, and the next I stumbled into one of the plain rooms of the temple. I caught myself and looked around. My friends were nowhere to be found, but I wasn't alone.

A gray-cloaked man sat in one of the simple chairs in the middle of the room. Beside him in a small wooden cradle lay a baby. He leaned over the cradle and smiled at the giggling baby. "You grow too quickly, Estelwen."

My eyes widened and my heart skipped a beat. I couldn't explain it to myself, but I just knew that that baby was me. My eyes swept over the young man with his short brown hair. Here, in the full flesh, was my father. His handsome features were no longer blurred.

"Dad!" I cried out as I rushed over to him.

Only I couldn't. I couldn't take a step toward him. My legs wouldn't move. I looked down at myself. My body was semi-transparent and my feet floated a few inches off the floor. I raised my hands and saw the floor through my fingers.

"Soon you will see your mother again. Would you like that?" my father cooed to my young self. I giggled and kicked my legs beneath the soft white blanket that covered me.

"Dad!" I shouted.

My father sighed as my tiny hand wrapped around one of his fingers. "I wonder, my little Estelwen, whether your mother isn't right in thinking I'm on the wrong path." He turned his face away from me and pursed his lips. "I think the brothers are hiding many things from me. Terrible things. Maybe the next time we visit your mother we will stay with her." He looked back at me and smiled. "Would you like that?" I giggled and bounced up and down. He laughed. "Then it's settled. The next time-" There came a knock on the door. My father pulled himself free of my tiny grasp and stood. "Come in."

Philo stepped into the room and closed the door behind him. He had both eyes and looked a little younger in dragon years. His face was grave as he clasped his hands together together behind him. "Good evening, Marcus."

Marcus furrowed his brow and took a step forward. "Is something the matter? Did one of the portal experiments go wrong?"

Philo sighed and shook his head. "Nothing like that, Marcus, but still I bring bad news."

My father frowned. My heart thumped in my chest. "What sort of bad news?"

Philo looked past Marcus and nodded at me. "Our Lord demands the child."

Marcus started back and his face paled. "Estelwen? Why would he want her? She is nothing to him."

"He sees potential in her," Philo explained.

My father shook his head. "Potential in a baby? That would mean he knew of her mother, and only you and I know-" His words caught in his throat as he noticed Philo's downcast gaze. Marcus took a step toward him and tried to catch his gaze. His voice was a mere whisper. "You told him?"

Philo swallowed hard. "I could not help it, Marcus. The Red Dragon needed to know."

Marcus turned away from him and looked down at me as I lay in my crib. His voice was low, but firm. "What does he intend for her? To use her as a battery, or to harness her mother's power through blackmail?"

Philo took a step toward him with his hand outstretched. "Marcus, you have to understand-" My father swung around and struck his hand away.

"I understand perfectly, my *friend*," Marcus snapped as he raised himself to his full height. "Your greed and ambition come before all else."

Philo cradled his hand against his chest and glared at Marcus. "Whatever you think of me, between us *you* are still the fool. You choose to deny our lord what he demands, and for that you have only yourself to blame."

A small, bitter smile slipped onto my father's lips. "Yes, we all make our choices. Your choice has given me only one for myself."

Marcus threw up his hand. A ball of fire erupted from his palm and slammed into the left side of Philo's face. The man screamed and clutched at his burning flesh. Marcus shoved him against the wall and scooped me out of the crib. He rushed from the room. The same invisible rope that held me in place now pulled me after him.

Marcus sprinted down the corridors of the temple with me tightly held against his chest. The sound of Philo's screams followed us down the hall. The dark torches that lit the corridor cast long, tree-like shadows over the walls. His breathing was labored as he carried me against his chest.

It was a reenactment of a terrible scene I had already witnessed, but with my vision now clear.

The little one that was me cried. My father slipped against a wall at an intersection and cradled me in his arms as he peeked around the corner.

"Do not cry, little Estel. Shh. We go to see your mother."

"Do you honestly believe she would be safe there?"

My father whipped his head up and I was spun around. Before us both stood the red-sashed dragon. He looked exactly the same, even down to the crooked smile on his lips.

The Red Dragon strode toward my father. A group of gray-clad brothers came up behind my father, but the sashed dragon held up his hand. They stopped even as he came closer to Marcus. "The Red Dragon's reach is far and wide. There is nowhere in this world where she would be safe."

My father frowned. "Then she shall be safe in another."

He threw his hand up in front of him. A black portal opened between the two men. My father drew me up and smiled at me. "Goodbye, my little Estelwen. May you live up to your name." He leaned down and pressed a kiss to my forehead. A faint glow of green sprang from where he touched me and sank into my head.

Marcus wrapped me tightly in the cloak and clasped me in both hands before he drew back his arms.

"Stop!" yelled one of the gray-clad men behind him.

Marcus hurled me through the portal. The gate shut slowly shut behind me, and my father looked to the red dragon. "Go in after her, if you dare."

The sashed dragon glared at him, and his eyes glowed a crimson red. "You are more trouble than you are worth, human."

My father smirked. "Wait until my daughter returns."

The dragon chuckled as he looked past my father at the other brothers. "You will not live to see that day." He raised his hand and snapped his fingers. The brothers fell upon him.

The same force that kept me in place drew me away from the scene as the world darkened around me. I was lost in a void. Lost and crying.

CHAPTER 28

My trip through the portal was short. The other end was also in another ceiling. Being the last one through the portal, I was also the last one out of it. I fell out of the portal and dropped onto a pile made up of Xander, Spiros and Darda. They groaned and yelped as my thin body dropped on top of them.

A shadow slipped over us. I was upside down on my back and tilted my head back to look up at the next danger.

Tillit leaned down and grinned back at me. "If I knew I was going to have company I would have cleaned up a bit, or maybe gotten a bigger room."

I looked around. We were in a tiny square room with cracked walls and a dingy curtain over the single small window. The darkness beyond the worn cloth told us that night still reigned. A bare cot and a nightstand were the only bits of furniture. Tillit's bag sat atop the cot.

"Miriam, would you mind removing yourself from my spine?" Darda pleaded.

I glanced down and saw my elbow was in her back. "Sorry!"

I climbed to my feet and the others followed. Xander leaned heavily against a wall in order to stand. I slipped around my friends and over to my dragon lord. "You okay?"

"I am, but you-" He brushed a finger against my cheek. "You have been crying?"

I winced and wiped my wet cheeks with my sleeve. "It's a long story, and if we make it out of this alive I promise I'll tell you it."

"I'd like to have a bit of the story right now," Tillit spoke up.

We brought Tillit up to speed, and at the end of our tale he gave a whistle. "My friends, you certainly get yourself into the worst of it. Fire-wielding brothers, Red Dragons, and secret tunnels beneath ancient temples."

Darda narrowed her eyes at him. "How do you know where the tunnels are located?"

He held up his hands and grinned. "Easy there, Darda. Tillit isn't the enemy. Besides, it's the only place it *can* be, and I've got a plan to get you back in there."

I choked on my spittle. "Get us back in there? Why?"

"Whatever they are planning, we must end it," Xander explained.

I whirled around and glared at him. "And how are you going to do that? There's about a thousand of them and only four of us."

"Five," Tillit corrected me.

I rolled my eyes. "That's really going to help."

He chuckled. "Well, if five won't work, what about fifty?"

We all turned to him with wide eyes. Xander arched an eyebrow. "Where can you get so many to help us?"

"Sinbad."

My jaw dropped open. "Sinbad? Seriously? He's the one who tried to get Xander killed in that race!"

Tillit held up his hand. "Hear me out. You told me it was Philo who put the Dragon's Bane in Xander, right?"

I nodded. "Yeah, but-"

"And it was the guards who helped keep you captive."

"Yeah, but-"

"So exactly why would they need Sinbad's help?" he pointed out.

I opened my mouth, but no words came out. I frowned. "Maybe, but-"

"He does have a point."

My face fell as I slowly turned to Darda. It was she who spoke. "*Now* you're agreeing with him?"

She pursed her lips. "Regretfully, I am. I can see no reason why they would use a poor Alfurasan Alriyah when they have the wealth and resources of the Temple."

"What about what that guy in the desert said? He said to ask Sinbad," I reminded her.

"Maybe it was a ruse to ensure we did not join forces with him," Darda suggested.

Spiros's eyes flickered to Xander. "But how can we be sure?"

Xander furrowed his brow and pursed his lips. He glanced at Tillit. "Can you arrange a meeting between Sinbad and ourselves?"

Tillit grinned and gave him a lazy salute. "Within the hour, My Lord."

"We need it within ten minutes."

The sus winced. "That's asking a lot, My Lord, but Tillit will see what he can do." He wiggled through us and slung his bag over one shoulder. "Just wait here and try not to destroy my room."

Xander grinned. "We make no promises."

Tillit slipped out of the room. I plopped myself on the cot and frowned at the floor. "I still think this is a bad idea. . ."

Xander seated himself beside me and smiled. "It is dangerous, but we have little choice." He looked up at Spiros. "How long do you believe it will take for the brothers and guards to find us?"

Spiros looked around at our quarters and shook his head. "That would depend on how Tillit acquired this room. If our enemies need to search the city house-by-house it will take some time, but if they know where this room is located then we can expect them in a few minutes."

Darda slipped over to my side and pursed her lips. "Should we not find another place to hide?"

"Not until Tillit returns," Xander told her. He looked to me and studied my face. "I am ready to hear your tale, if you are willing to tell it."

I sighed. "All right, but it's going to sound hard to believe."

He smiled. "That would be a tale worth hearing."

I took a deep breath and recounted what I had seen while going through the last portal. My companions were quiet for a moment after I finished my tale.

Darda seated herself beside me and wrapped her arms around me. "I am so sorry," she whispered.

I smiled and returned the hug. "It's okay. It's not like it was my fault or anything. But still-" I cast my eyes to the floor and fought back a few loose tears, "-I wish I could have stopped them."

"You may yet," Xander told me.

I lifted my eyes to him and nodded. "I know. By defeating them here, right?"

He smiled and bowed his head. "Ever the wit, my Maiden."

There came a tap on the door. We stiffened. Xander drew me against him as Spiros set his hand on the hilt of his sword.

"You can take your hand off your hilt, Captain Spiros," Tillit's voice called from the other side. The door creaked open and Tillit peaked his head in. "Ready for your meeting?"

Darda glared at him. "Must you be so annoying?"

Tillit opened the door wider and stepped inside with a grin on his face. "For you, any time. Now we should get going, but first-" he drew out five pairs of gray cloaks from his bag, "-disguises!"

CHAPTER 29

Tillit led us through the winding, night-shrouded back streets of Hadia to the very southwest point of the city. Xander walked behind him while Spiros brought up the rear. Darda was in front of him and behind me.

I looked at our motley crew of rumpled robes and pursed my lips. "Nothing suspicious about us. Just a sus, a couple of dragons and a human fae slipping through the streets in stolen priest robes. . ."

"They're not stolen," Tillit defended himself.

"Then how did you get them?"

"I bought them off the thief."

Darda glared at him. "That makes you an abettor of thieves."

DESERTS OF THE DRAGONS

"And a very good haggler," Tillit added. "He wanted a good fifty drachma for the robes, but I got him down to thirty-five."

"How much farther?" Xander asked him.

"Nearly there," Tillit promised as we slipped up to the wall that surrounded the city.

We crept in a northwest direction with our backs against the wall. Half a city block down we came upon a strange outline in the defensive structure. Tillit pressed his shoulder against the outline and pushed inward. The stone sank into the wall, revealing a hole. Our group slipped through the crack in the wall, and we found ourselves in an empty void. The boulders and bricks had long been hollowed out and replaced by a domed room. No natural light save from the entrance penetrated the depths, but torches attached to the walls illuminated the area. They provided the only light after Tillit pushed the entrance shut behind us.

At the far end opposite the entrance stood Sinbad with his horn blower, Wahid. The miraj driver sported a curved sword at his hip and a smirk on his lips. He made a sweeping bow to us as we approached. "Good evening, *Lord* Xander."

Xander stepped to the front of our group and pursed his lips. "Good evening. Do you know why I asked to meet you?"

Sinbad raised his head and nodded. "I do."

Xander's eyes wandered down to the sword at Sinbad's hip. "What have you to say of it?"

The young dragon chuckled. "Only that I wish it had been done sooner."

Spiros stiffened and grabbed the hilt of his sword. I balled my hands into fists and wished the room wasn't so dry so I could wipe that smirk off his face.

Darda glared at Sinbad. "How could you say such a thing? And we as guests to your uncle!"

Sinbad arched an eyebrow. "My uncle has nothing to do with this. It is a personal matter between the lord and myself."

Darda took a step forward, but Spiros grasped her arm. She still shook a fist at Sinbad. "Monster! Murderer!"

Sinbad frowned. "Murderer? Of what do you speak?"

"The thieves who attacked us in the desert inferred you were privy to their plans," Xander explained.

"And this is why you brought me here? To speak of lies and slander?" Sinbad wondered. Xander nodded. The young dragon whipped his head to Tillit and narrowed his eyes. "You swore to me he intended to honor me as the greatest of the Alfurasan Alriyah."

Tillit sheepishly smiled as he took a step backward. "Perhaps I misspoke just a little."

"Whatever Tillit told you to convince you to come here, his intentions were honorable," Xander spoke up.

Sinbad crossed his arms over his chest and frowned. "Did you lead me here to insult my name by attaching thieves to it, or was there more to this meeting?"

"The brothers and guards of the temple have betrayed their oaths of fealty and aligned themselves to the name of the Red Dragon," Xander explained.

Sinbad shrugged. "What is that to me and my men? The war against the Red Dragon effected only the cities of dragons lords and their servants, not the far reaches of the desert."

"It effects you now, and everyone in this world. They are experimenting with portals, and it is only a matter of time before they tear our world apart," Xander warned him. He took a step toward Sinbad. "My companions and I are outnumbered, and I am weakened by their Dragon's Bane. That is why we need the help of your men. Otherwise-" Sinbad held up his hand.

"Enough. You do not need to convince me with a plea. Anyone who interferes with a fellow Alfurasan Alriyah and intrudes on the sanctum is my enemy. They only made it worse for themselves by smearing my name." Darda and I grinned at each other. Spiros relaxed and Tillit leaned against the wall with a triumph smile on his face. Sinbad looked over our group. "Now what plan have you to find these defilers?"

"My Maiden and I were captured by them, but escaped. They held us in secret tunnels somewhere within the city. We must infiltrate them and capture their leaders," Xander told him.

Sinbad arched an eyebrow. "That is rather a vague plan. Do you even know how to access these tunnels?"

Xander turned to me. "Did you see the how we entered them?"

I shook my head. "No. I saw we were headed around the gate to the northeast, but then I got knocked out." My hand pressed against the round object in my pocket. I bit my lip. "What about going to there a different way?"

Xander pursed his lips. "I would rather we foresee where we would enter so we may escape the same way should something happen to you."

Sinbad frowned. "The whole of the northeast? That is a lot of ground to cover."

Tillit snorted and pushed off the wall. "Is that all? I can lead you to it no problem."

We turned to him. Darda glared at the sus. "How do you know the location of the entrance?"

He tapped the side of his nose and grinned. "This snout isn't just for looks. If a cart pulled by that many hadabs passed me I could follow that scent for a week."

"Do you intend for my men to fight their way to the leaders?" Sinbad asked him.

Xander shook his head. "No. We may need your assistance to enter the tunnels, and then you and your men would only be a diversion for any of the magic users who block our path. Otherwise it will be my companions and I who will face what danger awaits us."

"That's a lot of guesswork in your plan," Sinbad pointed out.

Xander grinned. "There is no glory without danger."

Sinbad grinned. "Well-spoken, Xander. After we have defeated these enemies and you have regained your strength we shall race again, and this time I will defeat-" A loud bang behind us made my group spin around.

The entrance shuddered under another blow, and the smell of smoke wafted through the cracks. Dust rained down from the ceiling as the room began to grow hotter. Some of the dirt hit the torches, casting part of the room into darkness.

"We have company!" Tillit yelled.

"Is there any other way out of here?" Xander asked him.

Tillit moved backwards away from the entrance and shook his head. "Never needed one."

Sinbad unsheathed his sword, as did Wahid. "This will be as good a spot as any to make a stand."

I drew out the Soul Stone and looked to Xander. "You're not going to argue now, are you?" Another blast of heat hit the other side of the door and shook the room.

DESERTS OF THE DRAGONS

Xander shook his head. "No, but where will you take us?"

I glanced over my shoulder at Sinbad. "Are your guys somewhere around?"

He nodded. "In the city, yes, but in the center of the pub district."

I snorted as I clasped my hands together and closed my eyes. "Of course they are. Come on, portal, do your stuff." The familiar green glow illuminated the dark room and everyone's face as they turned toward the light. The green glow burst from the stone and created my unique portal in the center of the room.

Sinbad's wide eyes stared unblinkingly at the portal. "By Alihat Dhahabia. . ."

I opened my eyes and grinned. "No, by-" A sudden wave of exhaustion swept over me. I clutched my forehead and swayed back and forth.

Xander wrapped his arms around me and looked down at me with pursed lips. "Are you well?"

I dropped my hand and smiled up at him. "I'm fine. Just a little dizzy, that's-" Another blast rocked the room. A quarter of the door exploded inward and peppered us with rocks.

Xander lifted his head and swept his eyes over our group. "Through the portal!"

They didn't need to be told twice as another blast flew off another quarter of the door. My companions rushed into the portal, but Sinbad and his man hesitated.

"What awaits us through this portal?" Sinbad questioned Xander and me.

Xander helped me over to the portal and looked over our shoulder where the remains of the door stood. I saw hints of gray cloaks and burning flames. "A better choice than what awaits us through there."

Sinbad pursed his lips, but rushed forward into the portal. Wahid was on his heels, and they disappeared together into the vortex. That left only Xander and me. One of the gray-lad men reached their hand through the hole in the entrance and raised his palm toward us. Fire burst from his hand and flew at us.

Xander grabbed my hand and pulled me into the portal. We slipped through the warm glow that resided inside my portal and flew out the other end atop a pile of broken furniture. I landed atop Xander who hit his back on the remains of a broken round table.

Darda stepped up beside me and helped me to my feet. I looked around and saw we were in something similar to Tillit's 'office,' a tavern with few windows and a lot of terrible smells. Most of those smells came from the group of men gathered around us. They were Sinbad's gang, the slippery snakes of the sand. Sinbad himself stood in the middle with his arms crossed over his shoulder.

Spiros helped Xander to his feet, and my dragon lord turned to face the glowering gang. Sinbad stepped forward and dropped his arms to his side as he met Xander's gaze. "Those were the enemies you spoke about?"

Xander nodded. "They are some of them, but there are many more."

Sinbad gestured to the men on either side of him. "My men are prepared to follow my lead, and I will follow yours. How can we rid our city and the deserts of these fiends?"

"We must rely on many of the traitorous brothers being out in the city searching for us. Your men will be a distraction for those who remain in the tunnels while we search for the leaders and capture them. Without their guidance I am sure the conspiracy will crumble," Xander explained.

"But how do you intend to reach these tunnels with the brothers about the streets?" Sinbad pointed out. His eyes fell on me and he nodded in my direction. "Can she create a portal to get us there?"

I shrugged as I pulled out the Soul Stone. "I guess I could try. It's worked so far." I clasped it between my hands and closed my eyes. There came the familiar soft heat from the stone, but this time I felt a tug in my chest. It felt like heartburn, but deeper. I winced and ground my teeth together. The glow from the stone penetrated my eyelids as it shot out and created the portal. The gasps around me made me forget the pain, but I couldn't keep back the fatigue that washed over me.

I swayed from side-to-side until Xander caught me. "Are you well?"

I smiled up at him. "I'm fine. This portal opening stuff takes a lot out of a girl."

"Perhaps you should remain here," he suggested.

I pushed his hands away and stood on my own two shaky feet. "And keep the home fires going? Hell no." I looked at Sinbad and his men, and jerked my thumb at the portal. "What are you waiting for, an invitation? Go kick some brother butt." A grin slipped onto my lips. "Just think of it as a reenactment of that battle a long time ago, but this time the brothers won't win."

Sinbad returned the grin with a sly smile of his own. "No, they will not." He glanced over his shoulder at his men and unsheathed his sword. "To battle and glory!" The desert men rushed headlong into the portal like a stampede of hadabs.

Spiros looked to Xander and smiled. "Shall we follow their lead?"

"Though perhaps not their enthusiasm," Xander replied.

Tillit hitched up his pants and grinned. "Then what are we waiting for?"

Darda glared at him. "You would be more useful in this bar."

He gave her a wink. "Now's my chance to prove you wrong, my dear Dard, so I'll see you on the other side." He strode into the portal.

Darda rolled her eyes. "He is impossible."

Xander grabbed my hand and smiled. "But he has the correct idea. Let us go."

The rest of us hurried through the portal and into the pit of danger.

CHAPTER 30

We rushed through the warm glow and landed on our feet on the other side. The familiar hard rock of the tunnel floor lay beneath us, and in front of us was a long, wide corridor with torches on the walls. The corridor stretched beyond my vision and was intersected by countless other halls.

Sinbad's men filled the hall, and he pushed through them to get to us. "Where do you need us?"

"Intruders!" a voice yelled. We looked down the hall and saw only Sinbad's men looking in the same direction.

"Part!" he yelled. They slammed themselves against either wall and gave us a full view of a red-clad brother. His arm was stretched backward and in his hand was a large ball of fire. "Swords!"

Sinbad's men drew their curved swords as the brother threw his fireball. The lead of Sinbad's men swung his sword downward and cut the flame in two. The fire flew in two directions and hit the wall. The impact caused a huge explosion that rocked the whole corridor and sent shrapnel over everyone. The front of Sinbad's group were blown back into the arms of their compatriots.

Sinbad swung his sword in the air and snarled at his own men. "Use your wings, you fool, and spread out!"

His men hefted their compatriots onto their feet and drew out their thick, pliable wings. They scattered in all directions and halls as the red-clad brother was joined by dozens of other bad guys. Each was armed with their own fireball power. Xander grabbed my hand and pulled me with him as he slammed his back into the wall.

I whipped my head to Xander. "How is using their wings going to stop the fireballs?"

He drew me against his side and smiled. "Do not underestimate the strength of the desert folk."

They lobbed their flaming artillery at us, and the chaotic scene got a little hotter. Sinbad's men drew their wings in front of themselves and angled their leathery appendages. The fireballs, being round, rolled up their wings while only scorching the thick skin. The men angled their wings so the fireballs rolled up and shot back toward their wielders. The brothers ducked and lunged out of the way.

Some of their fireballs got through the front ranks and hit the deeper rows of Sinbad's men. Others weren't so angled and slammed into the ceilings and walls. The corridor and ground shook, and pebbles rained down on us. The air became clouded with smoke and dust, but that didn't stop the fight. Fireballs flew past us and wings fluttered to and fro.

DESERTS OF THE DRAGONS

Sinbad slammed his back against the wall close beside us. One of his wings was scorched bad enough that smoke floated from his flesh. He clutched his wing and grimaced. "I do not know how long my men can keep these fiends at bay, so if you intend to find the leaders you should hurry."

Xander nodded. "We understand, and thank you."

Sinbad grinned. "Watch yourself. I still demand that race."

Xander smiled and bowed his head. "I will not." He looked to our group and gripped my hand. "Follow me."

He pulled me through the mess with Spiros, Darda, and Tillit at the rear. "Do you have any idea where you're going?" I shouted.

"Where the fighting is the fiercest," he replied.

"Oh goody."

We wound our way through Sinbad's men and took the first left turn into a narrower passage. More of Sinbad's men battled other brothers at the end of the hall. The blasts from the countless battles in the numerous hallways rocked the tunnels and shook the ground.

I lost my balance and fell into the wall on my right. "Are they *trying* to kill themselves?"

Tillit looked up at the ceiling and frowned. "Judging by the cracks I'd say yes. A few dozen more hits and this place could collapse."

Spiros looked to Xander. "That may be their design to destroy all of us."

A party of brothers appeared in a side hall close to us. Xander drew me behind him as they raised their hellfire hands. Another violent earthquake shook the corridor, and a huge crack opened up above us. Hundreds of gallons of pure blue water poured out of the hole and drowned the brothers. The downpour took them in a different direction even as some of its wet body crashed toward us. I shut my eyes and braced for impact.

The impact never came. I creaked open one eye. A wall of water stood from floor to ceiling only four feet away from us. I blinked at the massive blue liquid.

Tillit grinned at me. "Your powers seemed to have improved quite a bit since we were in trouble beneath the lake at Alexandria."

I shook my head. "It wasn't me."

Xander furrowed his brow as he studied the blue water. "I believe we have already made the acquaintance of our savior."

The waters stretched out toward us and formed the upper half of Alihat Dhahabia's body. She smiled at us. "I am glad to see you are all well."

Tillit hitched up his pants before he made a sweeping bow to the beautiful fae. "Good evening, my lady." Darda rolled her eyes. Alihat bowed her head to Tillit.

I stepped forward. "Do you think you could help us clean up these tunnels?"

She shook her head. "I am not allowed to interfere in the affairs of mortals except to protect myself and other fae."

I pressed my hand against my chest. "I'm half fae, does that count?"

Alihat looked past me at my friends. "I do not believe you need my assistance, little niece. I can see the resolve in your friends to protect you."

Xander moved to stand by my side. "My Lady Alihat Dhahabia, if you are not allowed to interfere with this battle might you give us your guidance? We must find the leaders of these traitors before they destroy your home."

She shook her head. "I do not know, but I believe your faithful priest may be able to locate them."

"Apuleius?" Xander guessed. Alihat nodded.

"Who isn't down here?" I quipped.

"I will provide you passage to him in order that you might save my pool from their destructive ways," Alihat promised.

Tillit grinned and tapped the side of his nose. "I like the way you think, My Lady."

The wily fae smiled and bowed her head before she drew herself back into the water. The liquid parted to create a narrow path. We rushed down the hall and followed the opening through the maze of tunnels. Though her water extinguished the torches, the glow from her clear water illuminated the path. Several dozen brothers met us at intersections and threw their fireballs at us, but the artillery hit the water and hissed out of existence.

The waters of Alihat receded just short of a large domed room. The back of a gray-clad brother stood in our path and blocked the entrance to the area. In one of his hands he held a fireball. Xander grabbed the hilt of Bucephalus and tensed.

A huge wave of water came from in front of the brother and slammed into him. His fire was extinguished, and he dropped backward onto his back. That gave us a clear path, and a clear view, of the room.

Apuleius stood in the center of the room. In both his upheld hands were round balls of water that swirled like the fireballs danced in the hands of our foes. He was soaked from head to foot, as was his followers who stood behind him in a circle. The old priest was breathing hard as his eyes flickered over the half dozen tunnels that led into the room.

His eyes widened as they fell on us. "Lord Xander!" We rushed over to him. Apuleius dropped his armed hands and extinguished his water to meet us halfway. He bowed his head to Xander. "You cannot know how grateful I am to know you are safe!"

"And I you, Apuleius, but how did you come to be down here?" Xander asked him.

I pointed at his dripping robes. "And how'd you get so wet?"

He sheepishly looked down at himself. "We had barricaded ourselves in the sanctum when the floor beneath our feet caved in. Lady Alihat drew us into her waters and set us down in these tunnels."

Xander pursed his lips. "So the traitors revealed themselves even to you?"

Apuleius nodded. "They did, My Lord, and we found ourselves outnumbered. I-" he bit his lip, "-I blame myself for not realizing sooner the threat within my own temple."

Tillit snorted. "It took you long enough."

Darda jabbed him in the side. "Hush, you."

I looked past Apuleius at his followers who still held their water balls. "So you guys could put out their fire all along?"

He nodded. "Yes. It is why they never attempted an open rebellion until their numbers were far greater than ours."

"Can you tell us where their leaders might be?" Xander asked him.

Apuleius glanced over his shoulder at one of the tunnels. "The most powerful of our enemies came from that tunnel. I believe they were a contingent of a larger group for many came at once and fought very hard against us."

Xander looked over our group. "Then we shall retrace their footsteps. The fight will no doubt not be easy. Are you all prepared?"

Spiros grinned. "We have come this far. Another fight will not be a problem."

I jerked my thumb at Spiros. "I'm with him. Let's do this."

Xander smiled and nodded. "Then follow me."

CHAPTER 31

We rushed down the corridor with Apuleius's group bringing up the rear. The tunnel narrowed and the ceiling overhead sank lower so that the tallest of our group brushed their heads against the rough stone. The air grew stale and dust tickled our noses and poked our eyes.

"This must be the most ancient part of the tunnels," Apuleius called to us.

"No kidding," Tillit quipped.

We ran into a large cavern and skidded to a stop. On the opposite side of the sixty-foot expanse was a single tunnel. Between us and the entrance were fifty brothers in red garb. They stood ten shoulder-to-shoulder and five deep. Their fireballs were at the ready in both their hands.

Xander glanced at Apuleius. "Can you manage them?"

DESERTS OF THE DRAGONS

Apuleius pursed his lips and shook his head. "I do not believe-"

The brothers didn't let him finish as they launched their assault. Chaos reigned as we leapt out of the paths of fire and dove against the walls. Apuleius's group returned fire with water, but merely extinguished half of the coming barrage.

Xander, Spiros and Darda went in for the kill. The pair of men ducked and dodged the artillery to get within swordlength of the leaders. They cut down the men, but were driven back by the rear guard and their scorching fireballs. Darda provided them cover with her daggers so they could beat a hasty retreat. The process was repeated, but very slowly as our foes became desperate in their throwing.

I looked around for a stone or stick. Apuleius's water would have been useful, but the fire being flung around evaporated those balls.

Tillit slammed into me and pushed me against a nearby wall as a fireball singed my hair. "Watch yourself, Miriam," he scolded me.

"I'd watch myself better if you could help me find something to fight with," I told him.

He looked over the walls. "You work with water, right?"

I nodded. "Yeah, but there's nothing here-" His piggish nose distracted me as it twitched and bounced. "What are you doing?"

"Follow me." Tillit moved along the wall, and I followed him as the battle raged around us. He stopped halfway between the two opposing sides and pressed his snout against the wall. His nose twitched against the wall for a moment before he leaned away and grinned at me. "It's right here."

I ducked a fireball and blinked at him. "What is?"

"This." He slammed his thick fist into the wall. The force of his punch pushed the wall inward and created a web of cracks. A small stream of water poured from those cracks.

I smiled at him. "Thanks. I guess Darda was wrong about you being useless."

He puffed out his ample chest and grinned. "Tillit's useful in any situation."

I cupped my hands together and let the water flow into them. My water dragon rose from the clear liquid and towered above me. I turned to the battle and grinned at the opposing army.

"Hey boys!" My call rang out through the cavern and made both sides pause. I held out the dragon in one hand toward our foes. My little pet thickened and stretched itself upward so that the spiky scales on its wet back brushed the ceiling. "Wanna play with this?"

Their eyes widened as they beheld the dragon. They stepped back and stumbled over one another. I looked up at my dragon and nodded at the men. "Go get 'em."

The dragon roared and flew at them. The traitors tossed their fireballs, but they were like pebbles thrown at a giant. The dragon rammed into the front of the group and swallowed others. The men floated down through the body of my dragon and came out the bottom soaked and unconscious.

"Together!" Xander called.

My friends and companions renewed their attack. The traitors were chopped down and knocked out, but even as we did battle more of our foes came. They paused just inside the doorway and beheld my dragon. The leaders cupped their hands together and created huge fireballs nearly as big as boulders. The heat from the balls was so great that I could feel the warmth from where I stood thirty feet away.

Our new foes threw their massive artillery at my dragon. The searing heat hit its body and sizzled the water. The dragon reared its head back and roared. I winced as a shot of pain rushed down my arm. The brothers kept up their barrage. Each new huge fire boulder left a hole in my dragon until he looked like swiss cheese.

The pain from my connection to the water beast was nearly unbearable. My dragon twisted and lashed about, crashing into the walls and ceiling. Dust and rocks rained down upon friend and foe alike.

I tried to get a handle on it, but the creature wouldn't obey. Tillit grabbed his bag and swung it just above my hands, severing my connection to the beast. The dragon disappeared.

My shaking legs collapsed beneath me, but Tillit caught me and lowered me to the floor. "You won't help anyone doing that," he scolded me.

I cringed and looked up. My friends were in the ranks of the new traitors. Their numbers dropped with each body, and soon only one remained. In his hands was the largest fire boulder yet seen.

He grinned at us and his eyes flickered to the ceiling. The man drew the boulder behind him and aimed the fire upward. "For the Red Dragon!"

A curved sword flew past us and embedded itself into the chest of the final brother. The man's eyes widened before the boulder in his hands disappeared and he dropped dead onto his back. I whipped my head in the direction from where the weapon had come.

Sinbad stood in the entrance corridor with a smirk on his lips. Behind him was a dozen of his men, Wahid included. They were scorched and blackened, but all had grins on their faces.

"You did not believe you could do this work without us, did you?" he wondered.

Xander hurried over to me and Tillit stepped back to let him look me over. "Are you harmed?"

I shook my head. "Just my pride."

"Xander!" Spiros called out.

We looked up. Standing in the opposite tunnel was another man in a red robe. His hood hid his face. The red-draped brother slipped his hand into his robe and drew out a curved sword. He raised the blade to his hidden face and stood still.

Xander pursed his lips and tightened his grip on Bucephalus. Sinbad strode into the center of the cavern and drew his own sword. "Allow me to handle a foe who fights with my weapon."

The two men squared off only three feet from one another. The first to make their move was the cloaked one. He jabbed. Sinbad parried. The clink of their two swords as they clashed rang throughout the cavern. Their movements were nearly identical down to the way their feet scraped along the rough floor.

The pair dodged not only each other but the bodies that littered the ground. Most would never rise again, but there were those I'd thrown unconscious. One of those decided to reach out and grab Sinbad's ankle. The downed man gave a yank and pulled Sinbad off balance, but not off his feet.

DESERTS OF THE DRAGONS

Sinbad's foe leapt forward and stabbed at our ally. Sinbad blocked the blow with a wing and, in the same motion, stabbed the fallen man in the chest, preventing any future interference. The standing foe shoved his blade deeper into Sinbad's wing and close to his chest.

Sinbad flung his wing open, flinging the other man's sword across the room. His disarmed foe stumbled back before he dropped to his knees and hung his head. Sinbad stepped forward and caught the stranger's hood with the tip of his blade. He flipped it back, revealing our foe. I gasped.

It was Tifl, son of Alzalam. Tifl lifted his head and sneered up at Sinbad.

Sinbad narrowed his eyes and lifted the point of his blade to his cousin's throat. "What is the meaning of this, Tifl?"

"It kind of makes sense, actually," Tillit spoke up. All eyes turned to him and he shrugged. "He'd know when the caravans left his dad's oasis and he'd have the money to pay off those thieves in the desert to do his dirty work."

Sinbad pressed the tip of his blade against Tifl's throat. A small line of blood ran down his neck. "You are to be the next shepherd of the oasis, and yet you would dishonor yourself through such treachery?"

Tifl sneered. "Do not be a fool. If a sandstorm comes, does the shepherd not hide himself alone in a cave if his flock will not follow him? The same is true of me. The sandstorm is the coming of the Red Dragon, and you are the flock too stupid to obey them. I am not so foolish."

Xander stepped forward and stooped. He grabbed the man by the front of his robe and lifted him off the floor. "What about your fellow followers of the Red Dragon? What do they plan for this world?"

Tifl smirked as he looked at Xander. "The end of the world, I hope." He bit down hard on his teeth. There was a soft crack as he opened a hidden vial inside one tooth. Tifl dropped backward onto the floor and his lifeless eyes stared up at the ceiling.

Sinbad pursed his lips as he sheathed his weapon. "May some goddess of the desert find mercy on your soul, cousin."

Xander turned to Apuleius. "Leave some of your men to watch over the wounded. We will go on ahead."

"I think there's safety in numbers," Tillit spoke up.

"My men will follow you," Sinbad offered as he stepped forward. "We will be your rear guard."

Xander pursed his lips, but nodded. "Then let us hurry."

We rushed down the final narrow passage. There were no side corridors and hardly any torches to light our way. There was soon, however, the light at the end of the tunnel. That was followed by the sound of many voices. They chanted in some obscure language that sounded familiar to my ears.

We reached the end of the tunnel and burst into another cavern twice the size as the last one, but without any other connecting tunnels. In the center stood a dozen people. Among them was Philo and the red-sashed dragon. Six red-robed men knelt on the ground facing the opposite wall. It was they who chanted the strange words.

He turned to us and smiled. "I congratulate you on reaching this point, Ferus Draco. My trust in the brothers of this temple were sorely misplaced." He looked past Xander at Apuleius. "You must teach your next group of brothers better so that I might have an improved army."

Apuleius glared at him. "I will never allow another to be led astray by your kind."

The dragon shrugged and shook his head. "What a pity, but I suppose I shall have no need of them soon."

Xander stepped forward and held Bucephalus in front of him. "What do you intend to do with these portals?"

The dragon chuckled. "Do you honestly believe I would divulge my plans to you?"

"You're a little trapped," Tillit pointed out.

The chanting brothers on the floor raised their hands in the air. A blast of air blew outward from them and pushed us back against the wall. The air that moved ahead of them swirled and formed itself into a giant black portal.

Philo grabbed the men and pulled them to their feet. "We must leave, brothers!" The group of red-robed men, Philo included, hurried through the portal. The last of their party to step up to the portal was the red-sashed dragon.

"Stop!" Xander yelled.

The dragon paused and half-turned to us. He smiled and tipped his head. "I am sorry to leave you without a proper farewell, but there are other things I must do. Please place a red rose on your mother's grave for me, will you?"

Xander growled and rushed forward. The agent waved to Xander as he stepped inside the portal. The swirling mass closed behind him and a moment before Xander's sword cut the sliced where it had been. He stood stiff and straight with his back to us.

I pursed my lips and crept up to him. "Xander?"

Xander swung around and grabbed my upper arms. The hilt of Bucephalus dug into my arm. "Open the portal! Open it and let us follow them!"

My eyes widened and I shook my head. "I-I can't. It doesn't work-"

"Open it!" he growled.

I shrank away from him. He released me with a push and glared at me with a mouth full of sharp teeth. "Open it."

I drew the Soul Stone from my pocket and grasped it between my hands. My hands shook as I closed my eyes and swallowed the lump in my throat. "Please let us follow them." The glow didn't appear. "*Please.*" Still nothing.

A hand settled on my shoulder. I looked behind me and found Darda smiling at me. "You have done enough. We should get you some rest." I looked past her at Xander. Darda followed my gaze and shook her head. "We cannot go any further."

Xander frowned and opened his mouth, but Spiros lay his hand on our dragon lord's shoulder. "She is right. Even if we could follow them it would be unwise. Wherever they have gone they have the advantage." He gestured to me. "And there is your maiden to consider."

At that moment the earth shook beneath our feet. Spiros caught me before I fell as rocks rained down on us from the ceiling. Cracks several inches thick ran from the floor to the tip of the dome above our heads. Several potholes opened up in the floor, forcing some of Sinbad and Apuleius's men to leap out of the way.

Tillit looked down the tunnel through which we came. He whipped his head back to us and his face was pale. "The tunnels are collapsing!"

Spiros looked to his dragon lord and frowned. "We need a portal, but not to follow the red dragon."

Xander pursed his lips, but glanced to me with softened eyes and normal teeth. "Make a portal to allow us to escape."

DESERTS OF THE DRAGONS

I stood on my shaky feet and pressed my hands together with the Soul Stone inside them. "I-I'll try."

Xander grasped my hands in his and looked me in the eyes. "Forgive me."

I managed a small smile. "Don't go saying any last words yet. Just give me some room."

The dragon men and Darda stepped back. I closed my eyes and took a deep breath. The stone in my hands warmed my skin and I felt a flourish of wind as the green and blue lights melded to create a portal. The fatigue stabbed me like a knife and made my body quiver. A sharp pain in my head made me wince, but I ground my teeth and scrunched my eyes shut as I focused on the heat in my hands.

"Move!" I heard Spiros yell.

I felt the rush of people as they hurried past me and into the portal. My mind began to grow hazy as my legs collapsed. A pair of strong hands grasped my upper arms and drew me against a strong chest. I didn't have to open my eyes to know that chest belonged to Xander.

I wasn't sure I could have opened my eyes, anyway. My body felt like a heavy rock as he rushed us through. The warm heat of my portal wrapped around me and lulled me into a deep sleep.

CHAPTER 32

"Estelwen. Estelwen."

My eyes fluttered open. I lay with my back on a cold floor. All around me was darkness except for the small area my body occupied. A shadow knelt beside me. They leaned into my light and smiled down at me.

"Dad. . ." I whispered.

My father cupped my cheek in his hand and nodded. "Yes, my beautiful little daughter. You did very well, and now you know who you are."

I swept my eyes over his handsome features. "Am I. . .am I dead?"

He chuckled. "No. This is a point in your mind where I placed a part of my soul to help guide you to your true self." He sighed and released my cheek. "But I cannot stay here any longer. I must leave you."

My heart skipped a beat. I reached up and grabbed his arm. "Please don't leave me. There's so much I want to ask you. So much I want to know."

He shook his head. His features began to blur, as did the darkness around me. "I am sorry, my little Estelwen. I have to leave you, but remember that you are not alone. You have your friends, and your mother."

My hand that grasped him fell through his arm. I sat up and tried to wrap my arms around him, but only his vague outline remained. "Dad! Don't go!"

"Goodbye, my little girl. Tell your mother I love her."

"Dad!"

I sat up and stared with wide eyes ahead of me. The familiar wall of the temple living quarters met my gaze. I whipped my head to and fro. There was Apuleius's table and chairs. Darda sat at one of them, but at my awakening she hurried over to the bed where I lay.

She grasped my arms and looked me over. "What is the matter, Miriam?"

I groaned and clutched my head. My body ached and my head hurt. I peeked open one eye. "What happened?"

She smiled at me. "You saved us all by opening your portal to the temple. Xander and the others are out now securing the grounds and accounting for allies and foes."

"How long have I been out?"

"Much of the night. The sun will soon be rising," she told me.

My face fell as I bowed my head. "Dad. . ."

Darda blinked her eyes at me. "What about your father?"

I shook my head and cleared some of the cobwebs. "It's nothing. I think I need to get up." I flung aside the covers and swung my legs over the side of the bed.

Darda set her hands on my shoulders and glared at me. "You will do no such thing!"

I smiled at her. "I'm fine, really. I just. . .I just need to go somewhere."

"Then I will go with you."

I shook my head. "I need to be alone. Just for a little while."

She pursed her lips, but stepped back to allow me to stand on my feet. "And if Xander wishes to see you?"

I stood and shuffled toward the door where I paused with my hand on the handle. "Tell him I'll be visiting with my aunt."

An hour later Xander found me in the ruins of the sanctum by the edge of the pool. The pool was cracked and dry. Not a drop of water remained.

Xander came up to my side and looked ahead at the pool. "She will return once the pool is fixed, though that may take some time."

"Because Apuleius lost so many men?" I guessed.

He nodded. "Yes, and the extensive damage to the foundation of the temple. It will take months to make the repairs, perhaps years, and even longer to dig out the tunnels and see if we might find clues to what Tifl and his ilk were planning."

I glanced at him. "How's Alzalam taking things?"

"He is a strong man, and Sinbad is by his side. Together they will be one another's pillar of strength," he told me.

"So what about the red robes that survived? Can they tell us anything?" I asked him.

Xander shook his head. "No one could have survived the collapse of the tunnels."

My shoulders fell. "So back to not knowing anything, huh?"

"I fear so." He studied me for a long while before he pursed his lips. "There is something I must speak with you about. I. . .I cannot apologize enough for my actions in the tunnel. It was wrong of me to demand that of you."

I shook my head. "It's okay. I mean, I really wish it would've worked. I don't know why it didn't."

"Apuleius has theorized that it must be a place you know personally in order for you to be able to reach it," Xander explained.

I snorted. "That would explain it. I guess I never would've been able to open it, no matter how not-tired I was, huh?"

Xander's face fell. "I am-" I held up my hand.

"Sorry, I know, but really it's okay. You weren't the only one putting us in danger. Remember how long I stood here asking the fae about my parents while you guys held the door?"

A soft smile touched his lips. "I do recall something of that matter."

I looked back at the ruined pool. "I. . .I saw my dad again. In that last portal. He said he needed to leave me, but I still had you to look after me."

"That will always be true," Xander promised.

I pulled out the Soul Stone from my pocket and looked down at its shiny surface. "Do you think it wouldn't mind me being selfish? Just this once?"

He arched an eyebrow. "Selfish how?"

I wrapped my hand around the stone and hugged it against my chest. "My dad took me to see my mom, so I should know where that place is. I. . .I want to know who she is. I want to talk to her about him, and about who I am."

Xander stepped forward and clasped his hands over mine. I looked up into his soft, smiling eyes. "That is not a selfish wish. If that would make you happy then I would wish it for you, as well."

I smiled. "Thanks." I took a deep breath and stepped backward away from him. "Now let's see if this works."

"Do you have the strength?" he asked me.

"If it'll find me my mom I'm willing to try. Besides, if I haven't been near her this won't work, anyway."

I closed my eyes and clasped the stone in my hands. I held my breath as I awaited the verdict of the stone, and nearly broke my concentration when the familiar warmth came forth. The strands of light slipped outward and developed into a small swirling portal.

I opened my eyes and looked to Xander. "Guess I might've seen her."

He nodded. "Yes. Let us see together who she might be."

He grasped my hand and led me through the portal."

CHAPTER 33

We stepped out into a different world. Gone were the bleak walls of the temple, and in their places was the majesty beauty of nature. Tall, ancient trees grew so close together that I could barely tell one another apart. Bushes with sharp thorns gathered close to the dirt trail upon which we found ourselves.

I turned in a circle and looked at our surroundings. A sight made me pause. Six tall towers stood above the trees a quarter of a mile off. I furrowed my brow. "This is-"

"The High Castle forest," Xander finished for me.

I looked to my left. The path led deeper into the woods. "Then that means my mother is-" I shook myself and turned to Xander. "Please stay here. This-" I glanced down the path, "-this is something I need to do alone."

He cupped my cheek his palm and turned so that I faced him. "So long as I live you will never be alone."

I set my hand on his and smiled up at him. "Then I guess you may as well come with me."

We walked hand-in-hand down the path and into the clearing. The air was calm and quiet. The soft pattering of the waterfall was the only sound as I looked up at Xander. He nodded and released our hands.

I turned to the pond and took a deep breath before I strode up to the edge. The water bubbled as it had on my previous visits, and she appeared. The Lady of the Pond. My mother.

The ancient fae was as radiant as her pond was clear, but her eyes were not as bright as times past. She stepped onto the stones in front of me and studied my face. "You know."

I crossed my arms over my chest and glared at her. "Yeah, I know."

"And yet I sense anger in your heart," she returned.

I snorted. "Geez, why would that be? Why would I hate someone for keeping something that important from me?"

She shook her head. "I could not tell you."

I balled my hands into fists. My body shook all over. "Don't lie to me! You could have told me everything the last time I was here! Hell, the first time I was here! So why the hell didn't you?"

She tilted her head to one side and a small, bitter smile slipped onto her lips. It was like the waning of a bright moon. "You were so naive. Not knowing what you know, not having seen the world that is half yours, would you have believed the truth?"

"You could have tried!" I argued.

She closed her eyes and shook her head. Little droplets of water fell from her long hair and dotted the water behind her like tears. "I did not dare reveal the truth to you while you were still so ignorant of this world. The risk that someone would have discovered your identity before you learned the truth was too great."

I threw up my arms. "But somebody *did* learn it before me! You failed and I almost got killed for it!"

She flinched. A ripple spread from just behind her and across the while length of the pond. Her words were like a whisper of a breeze across the surface of the water. "My beloved Mark, please forgive me." Tears of crystal blue slipped from her bright eyes. She half-turned away from me and shook her head. "You gave everything to protect our daughter, and I gave nothing."

My heart sank at the sight of such a beautiful creature wrapped in her own guilt. I swallowed the lump in my throat, but my voice was still a little hoarse. "Why didn't you help us?"

A bitter smile crept onto her lips as she swept her eyes over the meadow. "We Mare Fae are the most ancient and powerful of our kind, a pairing that is deemed a blessing on us by both fae and mortals alike. However-" she gestured to the woods, "-we are trapped. We cannot go beyond the borders of our waters. For some, that is a great distance. For others-" she dropped her hand and hung her head, "-that is a terrible curse."

I blinked at her. "So you can't leave here? Ever?"

She turned to me and nodded. "That is correct. Though you did not know yourself, you have braved dangers I could never fathom and adventures I will never know."

I frowned. "It hasn't exactly been a picnic."

She looked past me and smiled at Xander. "But you were not alone, and though you would despise me I am comforted that you will always be loved."

I flinched. "I-I never said that. I just. . .I just can't understand why you let us go back to the temple when you knew it was dangerous."

My mother's eyes fell on me and she tilted her head to one side. Her smile danced across her lips. "Your father was a stubborn man. He believed in his ideals would change the world for the better. My warnings about the true nature of the red dragons fell on his deaf ears, and he paid for his mistake with his life."

I bit my lower lip. "So that's it? We just have to accept that he made the wrong choice and had to die?"

She shook her head. "No. We accept that he made an unwise choice, but it was the red dragons who murdered him."

My shoulders fell. I turned my face away from her. "So what now? What's all this matter?"

She glided down to me and cupped my face in both her hands. Her warm touch soaked into me like a summer sun as she gazed into my eyes. "Now you will carry on the memories of your father as I have, and have many more adventures with your friends."

I searched her sparkling blue eyes. "And you and me?"

She smiled as she grasped my hands in hers. Her eyes never left mine as a bright blue light shone over our joined hands. "I will always be here when you need me, but I will leave you with this gift." She opened my hands so my palms faced upward. A large dragon rose up from my joined hands and stared down at me with crystal-blue eyes.

I furrowed my brow. "So I can make a bigger dragon now?"

"Focus on its eyes," she instructed me.

I looked into those dazzling orbs and a change happened. Starting from the top, the fluid skin of the dragon hardened into a crystalline armor that stretched down to my hands. The water dragon became that of ice. The early sun reflected off its scales and created a dazzling display of reflection.

"Wow. . ." I breathed.

"Now focus on your reflection within those scales," my mother told me.

I stared hard into the scales. My narrowed eyes stared back at me. Slowly my face became distorted and disappeared. The change was caused by the scales changing into a thick white mist. The mist curled upward like a pliable dragon and opened a fluffy-looking mouth to show off soft white fog teeth.

I looked across the fog to my mother. "A fog dragon?"

She smiled and nodded. "Yes. Mist and ice are both part of the domain of the Mare Fae, and now they are at your bidding.:

She drew away from me and back into her pond, releasing her hold on my hands. A sudden fatigue overwhelmed me and I was forced to drop my hands to my sides. The large misty dragon evaporated. Xander grabbed my shoulders and steadied me.

I leaned my head back and grinned up at him. "Neat, huh?"

He smiled and nodded. "Very neat."

I looked at my mother who softly smiled at me. "Thank you for showing me how to do that."

She closed her eyes and shook her head. "Do not thank me for those abilities. I merely brought out your potential."

I grinned. "I think I can safely say I inherited my potential from my mom."

"And your kindness from your father," she agreed.

"So is there any way I can make water out of thin air? Like the priests and brothers?" I asked her.

She shook her head. "No. We fae are bound to the natural forces in which we are immersed. Such a limitation was placed upon us by the elder gods so we would never be tempted to rule this world." Her eyes settled on Xander and her smiled wavered. "Please take care of my little daughter. She is all I have left of the man I loved."

He bowed his head. "I will care for her with my life."

"Hey hey hey!" I objected as I shrugged off his hands. I stepped between them and looked from one to the other. "I can help out with that, too, you know. I've got a misty dragon and an ice dragon and-"

"-and a penchant for trouble," he finished for me.

I crossed my arms over my chest and grinned at him. "I have a lot of help getting me into that, and getting me out."

"Always," he promised.

My mother drew further back into the pond and the soft blue glow around us began to fade. "Whatever your troubles, wherever your adventures, know that you are always together."

Xander and I turned to her. I gave her a small wave. "Bye, Mom, and thanks for everything."

She smiled and bowed her head. "Good luck, little Estelwen, my shining drop of water in the sea. Farewell, Lord of All Dragons." She dipped below the surface and the blue glow disappeared.

I looked up at Xander and arched an eyebrow. "'Lord of All Dragons?'"

He shrugged. "Only those within my realm."

I turned around and looped my arms around his neck. "So is this adventure officially over?"

He wrapped his arms around my waist and grinned. "I believe so."

"Good, because you owe me a vacation, a long one, and don't make me use my ice dragon on you."

He chuckled as he leaned down and pressed a soft kiss on my lips. "A long one. I swear it."

A pity he couldn't keep his promise, but we weren't going to know that until our next adventure.

A note from Mac

Thank you for purchasing my book! Your support means a lot to me, and I'm grateful to have the opportunity to entertain you with my stories.

If you'd like to continue reading the series, or wonder what else I might have up my writer's sleeve, feel free to check out my website at *macflynn.com*, or contact me at mac@macflynn.com.

* * *

Want to get an email when the next book is released? Sign up for the Wolf Den, the online newsletter with a bite, at *eepurl.com/tm-vn*!

Continue the adventure

Now that you've finished the book, feel free to check out my website at **macflynn.com** for the rest of the exciting series.

Here's also a little sneak-peek at the next book:

Island of the Dragon:

I leaned out on the railing of the elegant vessel and stared out at the calm waters of the lake in Alexandria. A cool breeze wafted by me, bringing with it the sweet smells of cooking and the sweet sound of children laughing as they raced along the shore following the path of the small ship.

I heard a flutter of sails and looked over my shoulder. Xander stood at the helm, and beside him was the captain, Magnus, and behind them was the first mate, the tall and pale Nimeni.

My dragon lord's eyes flickered between what lay ahead of us and the children that ran along the bank. He drew the ship parallel to the shore while the rough-cut sailors opened the sails to give the ship speed that matched the quick kids.

The outcropping for the temple of the lake fae forced us to turn left while the children scurried onto the thin strip of land. They hurried to the end and waved to us. I strode over to the railing and waved back.

One of the young lads cupped his hands over his mouth. "Lady Miriam! Come play with us!"

I glanced over my shoulder at Xander. "Can I, Dad?" I teased.

He smiled. "I hardly believe a mischievous Maiden like you deserves to play."

I climbed onto a box and from there onto the railing. The white water below me splashed against the waterline of the ship as though reaching out for me. "I'll take that as a 'yes.'"

I dove outward away from the rough waves and into the water. My water dragon drew out of my body and slipped beneath me so that I rode on its back. The children laughed and clapped their hands as I rode the beast to within a few yards of shore.

"I want a ride!"

"Me, too!"

"Please let me ride!"

I looked behind me at the dragon's long body and laughed. "I think there's enough room for all of you."

"Do you have room for one more?" a voice spoke up.

I looked past the children at a familiar figure that strode our way. I couldn't help but smile. "Were you the one who brought them here, Tillit?"

The sus stopped behind them and made a majestic bow in my direction. "I am guilty as charged, my fair Lady! I thought they might want a good swim before the water turns too cold."

I looked up and squinted at the overcast skies. "So does this world have Fall, too?"

"All the four seasons that yours does, My Lady," he assured me.

"Can we have a ride?" one of the kids pleaded.

"One last one! We promise!" another spoke up.

I patted the back of the dragon behind me. "Climb aboard. You, too, Tillit."

He picked up one of the smaller kids and waded into the water. "Much obliged for the honor, My Lady."

I grinned. "You won't think so when I'm done."

He set the kid in front of him and took a spot near the rear of my beast. "Surely you wouldn't be rough with children aboard, My Lady."

"Be rough, Miriam!"

"Yeah! We like it fast!"

I looked ahead and hunkered down. "Then hold on!"

My dragon sped forward across the surface of the water. Tillit yelped and grabbed hold of my beast as its lithe body slithered like a sonic-speed snake across the lake. We slammed through waves and skipped over rocks as we made our way along the shore. The kids cheered at every wave while Tillit winced.

The ride wasn't long. I didn't want to lose a passenger, or for Tillit to lose his lunch. Within a few minutes we slithered into shore. "All right, everybody off."

"Aah," came the collective sound of disappointment as the children slid off the back.

Tillit lifted his leg over the dragon's back and winced as he stumbled into the water. "A very exuberant ride, My Lady. You have great control over your powers."

I shrugged as I stood on my own two feet. "It's all in the-" My dragon slipped out from beneath me and knocked its tail against my legs. I yelped as I fell backward into the two-foot deep water. My head disappeared beneath the waves and my bottom hit the soft-stone floor.

I came up coughing and with my ears ringing with the sound of the kids' laughter. Tillit himself stood over me with a twinkle in his eyes and his hand extended. "Very great control."

"Ha-ha," I retorted as I took his hand.

He helped me to my feet and I, along with the children, stumbled to the sun-drenched shore to dry off.

"You dropped something," Tillit called out.

I turned in time so see him stoop and pick up a small book that floated beneath the waters. It was the shrunken tome given to me by Crates.

I felt the color drain from my face. "Oh shit!" I ran over to him and snatched the book from his paws so I could furiously try to wipe the cover dry with my wet shirt. "Crates is going to kill me!"

"Crates of the Library?" Tillit guessed.

I nodded. "Yeah. If he found out I ruined his book-" My breath caught in my throat as I recalled that terrible griffin and its merciless justice. I scrubbed faster.

Tillit yanked the book from my hands and smiled at me. "You have nothing to worry about, My Lady."

I stared at him with wild eyes. "Nothing to worry about? He's got a griffin that eats people. That's something to-"

"The book is dry."

I blinked at him. "Come again?"

He opened the tiny pages toward me and flipped through them. "See?"

I looked down and watched the dry pages flip over one another. "H-how?"

Tillit chuckled as he shut the book. "The Mallus Library hasn't survived this long without having precautions placed on all its books." He turned the book over in his hand. "I'd say with him knowing your powers he probably put a water-resistant spell on it." His eyes flickered up to me. "Though I am a little curious to know why you were keeping such a valuable book on you."

I breathed a deep sigh of relief and shrugged. "I asked some people in town if they could read it, but they couldn't even tell me what language it was in. Nobody seems to be able to read it, not even Apuleius."

"I can."

I arched an eyebrow at the sus. "Really?"

Tillit grinned. "Of course I can. I can't sell any books for a good price unless I know what's in them."

I nodded at the cover. "Then what's it say?"

He cleared his throat. "'A History of the Dragons By Crates of Mallus.'" He started back as the book expanded to its normal size. He rubbed his scrubby beard and furrowed his brow. "I think I just said the secret password to open this thing."

I grabbed the book and tucked it under my arm before I grabbed Tillit's hand and dragged him along the shore. The children followed behind us. "Come on. You're going to the castle."

He winced. "But My Lady, think of the children if you executed me!"

"An execution!"

"Wow!"

I snorted. "You're not going to be executed, you're going to read me what's in this book so I can find out why Crates gave it to me. Now stop squirming and let's get going."

Other series by Mac Flynn

Contemporary Romance
Being Me
Billionaire Seeking Bride
The Family Business
Loving Places
PALE Series
Trapped In Temptation

Demon Romance
Ensnare: The Librarian's Lover
Ensnare: The Passenger's Pleasure
Incubus Among Us
Lovers of Legend
Office Duties
Sensual Sweets
Unnatural Lover

Dragon Romance
Maiden to the Dragon

Ghost Romance
Phantom Touch

Vampire Romance
Blood Thief
Blood Treasure
Vampire Dead-tective
Vampire Soul

Werewolf Romance
Alpha Blood
Alpha Mated
Beast Billionaire
By My Light
Desired By the Wolf
Falling For A Wolf
Garden of the Wolf
Highland Moon
In the Loup
Luna Proxy
Marked By the Wolf
Moon Chosen
Continued on next page
Moon Lovers
Oracle of Spirits
Scent of Scotland: Lord of Moray
Shadow of the Moon
Sweet & Sour
Wolf Lake

Manufactured by Amazon.ca
Bolton, ON